T0270216

THIEVING SUN

THIEVING SUN

A NOVEL

MONICA DATTA

ASTRA HOUSE
NEW YORK

For information about permission to reproduce selections from this book,
please contact permissions@astrahouse.com.

Astra House
A Division of Astra Publishing House
astrahouse.com
Printed in the United States of America

Library of Congress Cataloging-in-Publication Data

Names: Datta, Monica, author.
Title: Thieving sun : a novel / Monica Datta.
Description: First edition. | New York : Astra House, 2024. | Summary: "A
    meditation on art, social mobility, debt, and the danger of using others
    to define our selves, Thieving Sun is about an obsessive first love affair
    and its tragic aftermath decades later that brings one woman's life in
    New York and pursuit of art into searing focus"-- Provided by publisher.
Identifiers: LCCN 2023037889 (print) | LCCN 2023037890 (ebook) |
    ISBN 9781662602573 (hardcover) | ISBN 9781662602566 (ebook)
Subjects: LCGFT: Bildungsromans. | Psychological fiction. | Novels.
Classification: LCC PS3604.A868 T48 2024 (print) | LCC PS3604.A868
    (ebook) | DDC 813/.6--dc23/eng/20231108
LC record available at https://lccn.loc.gov/2023037889
LC ebook record available at https://lccn.loc.gov/2023037890

First edition
10 9 8 7 6 5 4 3 2 1

Design by Alissa Theodor
The text is set in Sabon MT Std.
The titles are set in Rajdhani.

The sun's a thief and with his great attraction
Robs the vast sea; the moon's an arrant thief
And her pale fire she snatches from the sun.

—WILLIAM SHAKESPEARE, TIMON OF ATHENS, 4.3.432-434

But now? But now? The thieving sun touched Josephine gently. She lifted her face. She was drawn over to the window by gentle beams . . .

—KATHERINE MANSFIELD,

"THE DAUGHTERS OF THE LATE COLONEL"

Of [the Thing] Nerval provides a dazzling metaphor that suggests an insistence without presence, a light without representation: the Thing is an imagined sun, bright and black at the same time. "It is a well-known fact that one never sees the sun in a dream, although one is often aware of some far brighter light."

—JULIA KRISTEVA, BLACK SUN, ON GÉRARD DE NERVAL, AURÉLIA

TABLE OF ACCIDENTS

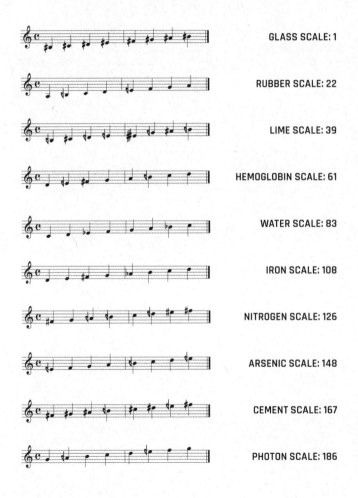

GLASS SCALE: 1

RUBBER SCALE: 22

LIME SCALE: 39

HEMOGLOBIN SCALE: 61

WATER SCALE: 83

IRON SCALE: 108

NITROGEN SCALE: 126

ARSENIC SCALE: 148

CEMENT SCALE: 167

PHOTON SCALE: 186

THIEVING SUN

GLASS SCALE

B ♮

There are times when I feel tired of this old world, Gaspar confessed that March from Damascus against the light of the mashrabiya. But they are rare. He had been there continuously since November except for a week in London at Christmas, which had turned out to be a strange place, he had said, once the Indian Ocean tsunami arrived. He turned off his laptop camera so that they were whispering to each other in the dark, as they had done every night since he arrived there, she past dusk and he near dawn. He was sipping something that rolled and gurgled with his saliva. The Syrian courtyard house was unique, he had assured her in the first week: it was studded with cornices—at which he had gestured—and not very tall, but the broken smudges representing the wave and motion of his hands on the screen blunted the view from his apartment terrace into the proprietor's courtyard, laid in warm stone and studied with mossy malachite fountains. Everything was lit with white flowers from the orange trees so that his own nose always felt stuffed up with plumes. He wished that Julienne were there: every morning he woke to the song of a copper workshop; she ought to hear them, he said. He wanted to record the craftsmen playing the material as instrument, etching and scuffing and stretching and brazing, he said; each sound was so supple: they worked with a pure, unstretched red material that did not gleam so much as radiate. He promised to bring some home. Their work softened the din of daily life in the medina, harmonizing all the sounds. One eased into the symphony till it became the ordinary fabric of air, although, Gaspar admitted hesitantly, he was beginning to feel that too many things had become air to him, which was not to call them ambience or static or white noise, not to discount vapor. Julienne was about to ask what he meant when she heard something burn and scratch his throat. Gaspar coughed and slurped again. Oh! he shouted. I've never shown you the morning light cast by the latticework; it's all petals, like Elysium—and when he switched on the camera the sun's angle cut the picture and the call went dead.

C ♯

Gaspar hadn't mentioned that Axel and Leïla would be sharing Christmas with them that year. Isn't that strange, Julienne had remarked. Not really, said Gaspar on I-84, long after he might first have brought it up. My mother loves Leïla; I think they have more in common with one another than we do. Julienne disinterested herself from the semantics of *we* and tried to enjoy the knot of traffic, which could be relaxing when she wasn't driving. Gaspar had returned a week earlier from Turkey, where he had been scoring a film; a stomach virus he alleged to have contracted beforehand had forced him to rush the work, and he had been, ever since, in a wretched state. The crackling signal from the World Service declared that forty people had been killed in two car bombings in Damascus that had been linked promptly to al-Qaeda. Well, that's a bold-faced lie, said Gaspar. His hands shook at the steering wheel. Do you want me to drive? Julienne asked. No, said Gaspar. When she tried to squeeze his hand, he slapped it to the wheel and looked impatiently over his shoulder. It was then announced that Kim Jong Il would lie in state till December 28. Václav Havel had been buried that morning. What a pair, Julienne thought, but she instead quietly switched to the classical station, which seemed only to play *A Charlie Brown Christmas* all month long. Secretly she didn't mind. Gaspar didn't say anything. It was clear and cold out. When they finally arrived at his parents' house, Axel and Leïla were already there. She was cradling a mug and wearing a thick light gray sweater, heavy dark blond hair held up by two chopsticks as if she were in an advertisement about crashing family holidays. Sana emerged from the study next to the living room and took Julienne's shoulders, brushing both cheeks with her own before wriggling her son into her arms. Leïla turned to Julienne. How was the drive? She asked. There was a lot of traffic, said Julienne, smiling politely. You're so funny, Leïla said with a laugh. This year you can be holiday orphans with us. Julienne, who had spent ten of the previous eleven Christmases with Gaspar's family, asked, Where's Ali? He went out to get more wine, said Leïla. For you, obviously; you know that he drinks very lightly. She paused then added, I mean, for you, and Gaspar, and for us, of course. In the living room, Axel, famously efficient in building fires, arranged logs. Isn't this the stuff of your Teutonic fantasies? Gaspar teased Julienne. They all laughed. How's your fellowship? Julienne asked Leïla, whose glass of something light red was fuller than she would expect from a woman with her wine pretensions; also, where had the mug of tea gone? I'm enjoying it, said Leïla, but the commute is terrible, the train and then the Dinky. Academic museum culture is so stilted: I always feel better returning home to the city. Still, I've been allowed into fascinating conversations. Besides, I can do what I want with the place: it's full of walking mummies with excessive tenure who salivate when I come in, waiting to be told what to do. Sana knows what I mean. Sana brought up a mathematics lecture that had suggested that some thinkers were birds (Descartes) who thought broadly and others were frogs (Bacon) who concerned themselves with details. We're all birds here, said Leïla. Except for Julienne, of course. Bacon was brilliant, Sana insisted. Just then Ali, who had gone straight to the kitchen upon return from the wine shop, surprised them all to say that dinner was ready: a ghormeh sabzi had been simmering on the stove all evening, perfumed with dried black limes. Taste, Julienne thought: this had drawn her to Gaspar himself, who had a sense of aesthetics one could not gather from his persona, unlike the vulgar Leïla. It sounds like the academic curators are really falling in line, Leïla, said Julienne as they took their places around the dining table. Intern today, lead prosecutor tomorrow—what can't you do? Leïla said, Apparently I don't know how to use the correct plastic spoon; Julienne and I went for coffee and a walk last month and she gave me such hell for using one to stir in my honey. No, said Julienne. Just use the swizzle sticks; no need to waste a plastic utensil clearly designed for soup. Leïla sighed. We don't have these things at home. Bâtonnets, said Ali. Ah, said Leïla. Do they look so different, asked Julienne, smiling tightly. Should they be made from plane trees? Leïla laughed and said, Julienne is the funniest person I know. Oh no, said Julienne. I forgot toothpaste. I brought toothpaste, said Gaspar. We all have toothpaste, said Leïla, cackling, unless there's a homeopathic marigold powder you prefer. It's a prescription, said Julienne. Naturally, after a lifetime of poor dentistry. I'll just be a second; the pharmacy counter will close soon. Gaspar, who knew she was lying, did not follow.

D ♮

Julienne hadn't heard anything from Leïla in nearly two years. Past midnight one night she received an email inviting her to a baby shower and promptly burst into tears. The next day, in her second session with a therapist she had chosen at random from the insurance directory, she recounted this reaction. Maybe they were tears of joy, said the therapist. Julienne decided not to see her anymore. Some Sundays later, the shower took place. Everything from the online registry had been taken. There was a store for babies near Leïla's new condo in Tribeca; Julienne saw a stuffed giraffe but worried about SIDS. She purchased a set of glass bottles, a jar of shea butter, and a puffy Italian alphabet book and had them all wrapped in billowing paper. When Julienne arrived at the building the concierge directed her to the rooftop. There was a glass-walled lounge that separated her from the roof terrace. There were at least ten babies present. She tried to open the door but it was locked and required fingerprints. She waited till a group of people left. They dropped the door behind them instead of holding it open or even passing it to her, something that had rarely happened to Julienne till recently. She saw a heap of gifts and added hers to the pile before scanning the room. She could not recognize anyone there but for Leïla and Axel, costumed in brocades and silks—the event, Julienne presumed, would include a ceremony of ancient significance; no pastel confetti for them—and surrounded by expensive-looking older adults likely to be the future grandparents. There was no wine. Julienne found some plain sparkling water. She recognized someone smiling and walking toward her. It was the other Gaspar, the Danish archaeologist of the Andean Preceramic from the empty department at Princeton. It's been such a long time! he said, kissing her on both cheeks. How are you? he asked. I'm doing well, said Julienne. Where are you these days? Oh, you know, said the other Gaspar. Everywhere and nowhere. Quite tired. How about you? Just here, said Julienne. We are debating whether Leïla's pregnancy will be more like Beyoncé's or the royal baby. Julienne said, We can't know the details. The other Gaspar laughed. By the way, he said, have you recently spoken with Gaspar? No, said Julienne. How is he? Very well, said the other Gaspar. I think he enjoys living in Oslo. Julienne inhaled water and began to cough. When she came to she asked, Oslo? What is he doing there? The other Gaspar said, One of his pieces was performed in a festival at the opera house there and he decided to stay. Detecting something in Julienne's expression, the other Gaspar interrupted himself. I'm sorry—I thought you knew. We haven't been in touch, said Julienne. The other Gaspar nodded. It's difficult. Julienne asked, How is he?

The other Gaspar hesitated before saying, He's doing very well, he came to Copenhagen in wintertime when I was home. Oh, all right, said Julienne. He married a Norwegian woman, the other Gaspar blurted out. What? Julienne demanded. She worried that she might be heard but it was quite loud. The other Gaspar apologized again, shaking his head like a Muppet. What a terrible way to find out. Still, I think that you should know. It's fine, said Julienne, locking her jaw into a polite smile. One of the singers? she joked. The other Gaspar nodded. Her name is Mina. Julienne's brain rejected the information out-right: Gaspar, married, Norway, Mina with lungs. But what about Los Angeles? Julienne asked. What happened to his job? He goes back and forth, said the other Gaspar. A good sleeping pill on SAS. I see, she said. Mina is also the daughter of a famous architectural theorist, the one who has been promoting the notion of landvættir in public space. Isn't that strange? What's—oh, never mind, said Julienne. Yes, it is crazy! said the other Gaspar, laughing. I mean—it's not important, said Julienne. Do Norwegians normally get married? I don't think so, said the other Gaspar. It was something he really wanted to do.

E ♮

I could not stomach you when we first met, so awkward, so disorderly, even slightly icky, although you were much more hygienic than the undergrad boys and smelled of olive oil soap, the fruit and herbs you liked to cook with, generic laundry detergent. Sloppiness had always offended me. I associated it with ignorance, carelessness, inertia, the way that hatred grows, of degradation, something I would not understand acutely until you died at your own hand. Your legible disorder in the literal sense of that word and not the pathologizing of what ended your life had the soft, scratchy warmth of a vinyl record, in which an object of odorous synthetics becomes identified with organic qualities and Proustian memory. Despite your surface imprecision you turned out to be the most mentally organized person I had ever known. This was not to say that you had a superb memory but that everything was its place. I didn't understand this when we were very young, only that you never seemed to lack the correct thing to say. You could leave everything to the last possible second with few consequences, an intuitive calculus that never seemed to accumulate: that was for me, condemned never to forget. You, on the other hand, sprang off the walls like an electron, scattering wasted energy, or jewels.

F♮

They were eating at a new Thai restaurant in Prospect Heights from the same owners of the obnoxiously good— Bob's words—Thai restaurant in Woodside. Julienne was trying not to wince at Bob's slurpy, sweaty soup noodle eating skills: there were bits of noodle, napkin, fishcake, striated meat muscle, or all the above mashed into his beard. Tell me about him, Bob said. What? Julienne asked, pretending not to hear him over the racket. Gaspar, said Bob. No, she said. I don't want to discuss it. He said, You spent more than a decade, your whole adult life with this guy, and then he died. You're allowed to feel sad. Julienne said, I can't call this sadness or even depression. It feels like swimming in rubber sap, hardening slowly but for eternity, dense and stretchy all around but with no give. Bob laughed. Julienne said, he took his own life. He looked around at the world he loved—did I tell you he had a son—and decided that it would be so much better without him in it that he committed a violent act of murder against himself, however he did it. Bob asked, Do you think it was Norway? What? Julienne again pretended not to hear him. All the cold and dark, he continued. She said, I think that he suffered from depression his whole life and in winter exile had nowhere to go but inward, which became a worse and worse place to be. Did he try meditation? he asked. I'm a sixth-generation Norwegian and every year it's kind of miserable in Duluth. Julienne said, He was far away from anything he cared about. Other than his wife and son? Bob asked. His parents, who were very close to him, said Julienne, and Syria, of course. I just don't buy that the war could be the cause of his suicide, said Bob. Fine, Dr. Kierkegaard, she said. If only he had a SAD lamp. Wasn't he Danish? he asked. She said, I'm struggling with my role in his unhappiness. That's narcissistic of you, he said. Obviously the guy had a lot of problems. Julienne sighed and opened her wallet to take out three crisp twenties, which she set on a clean napkin before placing them on his side. You've hinted that I never get the check, she said. He apologized. No, I'm sorry, she said, standing up. I have a headache. She walked out as peacefully as possible, thanking the staff, found a green taxi, and began to sob before she could say a word. The driver opened the glove compartment and offered her a packet of tissues. Are you all right? No, said Julienne. My friend killed himself. The driver said, I'm sorry. Thanks, said Julienne. It happened to a good friend of mine when we were children, the driver continued. She had always been very sick but developed a problem with her esophagus. The doctor had replaced some of it with rubber and plastic tubing; medical facilities in our village were limited. Even fifty years ago this was not an ideal solution. She never got better and then smelled badly; her skin would peel away, in pieces. She was the eldest girl in a large family, with a horrible mother who would come to school at day's end and strike her in public for the most minor of domestic violations. Everyone would wait for them and laugh. One day she came into the chemistry laboratory. There was no reason for her to be in it, as she was studying home economics. She took something and ran out of the room. I chased her all the way down the hall—I didn't like stealing!—and demanded to know what she held in her palm. She refused to show me and ran from the building. The next day we learned from the teacher that she had died. It must have been the acid that she took from the lab. I asked whether there should be a moment of silence in her memory. The teacher said that because the girl stole and because she took her own life that she did not merit one. But such a loss remains somewhere in the bones as long as you live, as it should.

G ♮

After years of fetishizing both the act and object of drawing, this year she would learn to draw for real. Her sketchbooks often embarrassed her, although a five-year statute of limitations applied; she now enjoyed looking at her thoughts from graduate school. The drawings were more like process diagrams than rough sketches and her line work was fine and delicate. Of course she had taken the fundamental drawing courses in college and had been an adequate renderer of flat life but did not know how to turn paper into flesh, smudges into blood, strokes into breath, and even the notion of all this felt silly and embarrassing to her. She went to the Art Students' League, now in the shadow of a wavy obscene gesture slash billionaires' tax shelter best known for its many construction accidents. Julienne signed up for twice-weekly sessions; the instructor attended only one of them. Otherwise the students sat in a circle squinting intently at the model. She had been posing for decades, fine silver curls floating above the ears like a halo, a dancer's posture, orbs of mole and freckle. She was heavy and steady on the creaky joke of a stool as if it were the only place for her. Julienne mapped out the proportions as if the model were a wooden mannequin and swept in musculature. That isn't bad at all, said her neighbor, approvingly.

A ♮

When her year in Germany ended, another study-abroad student suggested that Julienne should look for a ticket from Europe to America rather than one from Berlin to Newark. The cheapest flight Julienne could find was on Aer Lingus, from Dublin to Boston. Julienne's first-year roommate, Jennifer, lived with her parents in the suburbs and offered to let her stay the weekend. They would meet for dinner after Jennifer finished her day interning in a department of hematologic oncology. Julienne took the airport bus into town, locked her large suitcase at South Station, and then went to the ICA, a flat white box on Boylston Street. Travel weary, she sat on a bench to watch some video art screened at the Venice Biennale. A short film from somewhere in the Nordics depicted a group of friends walking in a boreal forest on a frozen lake. One comrade mused, What would happen if the ice gave way and we all fell in? Another responded, softly, The shock of the cold would make you hyperventilate but instead of air you would inhale icy water. A second said, Your arteries would constrict in response to the cold, making blood circulation more difficult and a heart attack more likely. Still another said, decreased blood flow incapacitates the arms and legs. You will then succumb to hypothermia without a flotation device, followed by cardiac arrest. The one who posed the question expressed relief that this was not going to happen. And then it did: all six of the friends fell through the ice, froze, had heart attacks, and drowned. When Julienne told Jennifer about the film over dumplings and beer— their first legal one together—she nearly suffocated from laughter in response. This was a movie you saw? she asked. Voluntarily? Some video art at a museum, said Julienne. But is it accurate; is this really what would happen in that situation? Jennifer said, I'll consult a polar lifeguard.

B♮

Gaspar had returned home from Syria a week earlier and was still slightly jet-lagged. Punctuality had still never been his strong suit: often he teased Julienne for having an internal atomic clock. Before leaving the office she called their home answering machine to learn that Gaspar would be fifteen to twenty minutes late (forty, she reckoned) because he was helping a friend start his car in a parking garage in Chelsea so that they could take it to a mechanic. She shook her head at this story and decided not to ask him about it in front of Leïla, the friend of Gaspar who knew him best—After you, of course, he had interjected to Julienne—and he would disappear a little when she called from France or Tunisia or Neptune, ducking and whispering hysterical laughter into the receiver from either side of the bookshelf that divided their sleeping area from the kitchen. Tell me about her, she had said. She's from a family of diplomats, said Gaspar, except for one of her cousins in Toronto who does stand-up comedy. Nor her, said Julienne. Not yet, said Gaspar. They had become fast friends on a summer Arabic language fellowship in Beirut and were since inseparable. Well, not recently, Gaspar explained, because they hadn't lived in the same country since undergrad. She was repatriating (well, sort of; she grew up in Paris, he added) to start a doctoral program in art history. Leïla specialized in French romanticism, aspects of which she found tiresome, racist, and sexist, but she always remained very radical, never reductive, in her critique. You'll like her, he had insisted to Julienne. She also studied art history and is an amazing painter. Why am I learning all this now?

Julienne had asked. Gaspar had apologized. Now she was waiting for him, and Leïla, and Leïla's Swiss husband, Axel, at a Luxembourgian fusion restaurant in the West Village. Julienne was ten minutes early—the correct time to arrive in most situations, she had tried to teach Gaspar—and ordered a martini with lemon at the bar that from thirst in the dry winter heat she drank too quickly. There was a man at the stool on the other side of her handbag reading something slender whose cover she recognized from work: some of the other administrative assistants were reading the same book. Excuse me, she asked in German, are you reading *The Unpleasant Things First*? By Sibylle Berg? Yes, he replied. My sister gave it to me. It's very silly. I'm told, said Julienne. Are you Axel? He said, Yes. You must be Julienne—I've heard so much about you. Me too, fibbed Julienne. Why do you speak German? Axel asked. I studied in Berlin and work at a German Landesbank, she said. They have one in New York? he asked. At least two, she said. Just then a petite figure scented in a veil of white flowers bounded from Julienne's periphery. Hi, I'm Leïla, she said, reaching gracefully to Julienne's shoulder and brushing her face lightly on the cheek in a way that made her feel like a giraffe. Leïla recovered more quickly from the exchange than she did. You must be Gaspar's partner, she said, a term that Julienne did not yet know applied to straight girls her age. We've heard so much about you. Julienne ordered a second martini. Gaspar burst through the door, literally running, wearing a hooded sweatshirt adorned with blue kittens in puffy glow-in-the-dark paint that he had described as sick. Hi! he said, greeting everyone, including Axel, with a kiss on the cheek. Has everyone met? Leïla and Axel excused themselves outside for a cigarette. Julienne said, You arrived at exactly the twenty-minute mark. Gaspar said, I said I'd be late. She said, You can't expect everyone to wait for you. He said, I'm Julienne, and I'm so punctual. She said, I'm Gaspar, and time moves twice as slowly for me and only me because I am twice as important as everyone else. Gaspar said, That's not fair. Julienne said, I'm Gaspar and I can dish it out but I can't take it. She laughed, accidentally splashing him in the acid of her martini from the barstool perch, and when he blinked, stung, she laughed again.

RUBBER SCALE

A

The floor at Julienne's ballet school was slightly bouncy with a glossy gray coating that allowed them to slip. Sometimes before the teacher arrived the girls would perform what they considered to be superhuman gravity-defying gymnastic feats. She sensed even as a child that there were certain acceptable ways of enjoying oneself in ballet class—the perfection of form, expression through music, articulation of the human drama—but to be polite and not to appear odd to the other kids,

Julienne would turn a few cartwheels or lean backward into a bridge form so that she could kick her legs over her head and return to a standing position. But these were not the things for which she would be rewarded. Her mother, Willa, had enrolled her in lessons when she was three years old (she did not realize that she could simply stop going until she was in high school), but by the time she was six, Julienne looked forward to them; the studio was a place of peace where her natural tendencies and form were exalted: she was precise in her movements but not rigid, limber but not in a grotesque double-jointed Gumby way, graceful but not fussy, tall but not lanky, talented but not so much so that she might sacrifice her bloodied feet at the altar of Balanchine. She attracted both admiration (lead roles) and contempt (being called Little Miss Muffet) in the studio and it embarrassed her to be held out as an example because she was not sure what she was doing that gained so much approval; she maintained simply that if one could not perform a plié correctly, one was not performing a plié.

B ◌

They had spent most of winter break bouncing between the floors and sofas of friends. Gaspar had invited Julienne to his parents' house for Christmas, and also to request the key to their old apartment on the Upper West Side. (Bound for Hawaii, Willa did not object to her daughter's absence.) The house in central Connecticut was angular and unimposing with an exterior free of decoration, which, having been built in the twentieth century, meant it was both tasteful and costly, as Julienne had learned in her History of Decorative Art class. Gaspar had said that his father, Ali, was an architect from Iran who taught at Yale. His mother, Sana, was a mathematician from Iraq who taught at a small liberal arts college like Julienne's. They had met in graduate school in London, where Gaspar was born and had lived till he was eight. Julienne decided not to ask him whether the Iran-Iraq War had produced domestic discord. Gaspar had a house key but rang the doorbell anyway, and when Sana opened the door, she greeted him as if they had been separated for decades. Mom, this is Julienne, he said as she led them into the house. Hi, said Julienne, who did not know what to call Sana. She had probably kept her name. Hello, said Sana, running water into a kettle. She asked Julienne how she knew Gaspar. I'm an undergrad at the College, she said. Sana nodded and asked Gaspar questions to which she may have already known the answers: Had he heard anything from doctoral programs, and were all of his applications in? How was the new composition? How was the distinguished so-and-so with whom Gaspar was studying? When would the production open? Was he eating well? Over tea and biscotti, Gaspar tried to tell Sana things about Julienne. She was from New Jersey. She had spent the previous year studying in Berlin. She was studying art history and sculpture. She was good at math. Sana nodded and excused herself to grade papers, disappearing down a hall into sun and shadow too far away for the audible click of the door. Gaspar said, Would you like to see the embarrassments of my childhood? Julienne nodded. He pulled her up by the hand and took her to a room upstairs, with a dormer window facing the street and a skylight in the mono-pitched roof as well as a window seat facing the yard, which held a treehouse, a greenhouse, and a gazebo. The walls were linked with built-in bookshelves, cupboards, and drawers that blended into white oak walls. This is very tasteful for a kid's room, said Julienne. My mom took down the Transformers posters when I went away to school, said Gaspar. I never truly forgave her. The books seemed to have been arranged chronologically in the order Gaspar had read them, with children's books on the far left and hulking reference materials on the far right. A large, elaborately bound volume stuck out from the shelf after the Richard Scarry anthologies. When she took it down, Gaspar said, Ugh, please don't look at that. It's not your diary, is it? she asked. He said, When I was a baby, my dad wrote out and illustrated the story of Gaspard de la Nuit. He never sent it out or anything. He felt it was best kept private. Julienne sat on the floor and opened the folio. Every page was beautifully calligraphed and burst with lively watercolor. They really love you, Julienne observed. Why do you say that? Gaspar asked. She shrugged. They spent the afternoon in his childhood bed with its many utilitarian storage elements, about which Julienne could not stop wondering.

At dinner Julienne met Ali, more effusive than Sana; for instance, he asked her to call him Ali and expressed admiration for Anselm Kiefer, about whom Julienne had read in her German Expressionism class. At dinner there were brussels sprouts with bacon; it had not occurred to her that Gaspar's parents ate pork. Look at that, said Sana. Julienne holds a fork so beautifully. Julienne felt ashamed and looked at the others' hands, but they were all drinking water or wine or dunking bread. What do you want to do after you graduate next semester? Ali asked. Julienne said, I've been thinking about law. German Expressionist law? asked Sana. What do your parents do? My mother works for an airline, said Julienne. And your father? asked Ali. I don't know, said Julienne. Bolstered by liquid confidence and diminished appetite, she said, He was a stranger my mother met on a transpacific flight. Fascinating, said Sana. I know only what she told me about him, Julienne continued, and no more. What did she tell you? asked Ali. Only that he was a surgeon from Hong Kong, said Julienne. They agreed not to tell one another their names. Are you joking? Sana cackled. No, said Julienne, maintaining eye contact till

Sana looked away. Only later would she understand that she had lost.

C

They tried to open all the windows when the air-conditioning blew its fuse, but the outdoor temperature was too high. Juicy mosquitoes hovered over the window unit in the bedroom. They then slammed shut all the windows to muffle the voices of sweaty grumbling from the street and the tranquil fire escape, from which one could sometimes hear a choir or piano, but which today let in the scents of hot garbage, tuberose, and a botched barbecue of blood sausage and kidney, according to Gaspar, who had a perfumer's nose. He angrily poured himself the last of the Chartreuse brought home from the Festival d'Avignon and shut himself in the spare bedroom that had become his workspace. Julienne, no longer able to distinguish these summer obligations from one another, was content to cede him solitude until she smelled smoke and plastic. A moment later he burst into the living room to take away the fan. She began to ask if he was all right, but Gaspar brushed past her without a word in the hallway, gently bumping her shin with the fan's feet, and shut himself in the study again. She took the fan from the bedroom and lay on the sofa with a cool khadi sheet draped over it and began to dream about the Palmyra mountain belt Gaspar had told her about till she woke to the awful tinny humming in her ear and wet welts on her arms. She balled up the cotton cover to take to the laundry, where there was also no air-conditioning, but at least it was not home.

D

Leïla and Axel were in town from London, having traded apartments with Gaspar for a few weeks. They invited Julienne to dinner at a Puglian pop-up restaurant in Williamsburg, for which she was a touch late after a solo double bourbon next door. She had met everyone over the years except for a masseuse and photographer introduced respectively by a philosopher of Borromean rings and a scholar of Flemish performance art as *my next of kin* and *my lover.* There was a postdoctoral couple from

Sofia and Oxford presenting at the same conference on historical materialism, at which most of the others were in attendance, but it was not the conference on historical materialism (London, early November). The rest were hatchling faculty from the academies of the American northeast, most from Leïla's doctoral program. Everyone had slept with everyone else and had been analyzed by the same Lacanian. Gaspar's sudden absence made Julienne at once dull and dangerous: women sized her up as they talked over her; men avoided her gaze in front of their partners but looked her up and down when they stepped out for a smoke. Regretting the brevity of her dress, she ordered a glass of the Barbera, which Leïla said came from subpar terroir and in this case she would recommend Negroamaro or Sangiovese, and Julienne had to tetanus-lock her jaw into a smile to keep from lunging across the table and shaking her by the shoulders. She also ordered pappardelle in lamb ragù. She excused herself to wash her hands for twenty seconds, then re-spackle in the colors of prophy paste green then dental ceramic a vermilion cyst, then wash her hands again for twenty seconds before applying moisturizing cream and hand sanitizing gel. When she returned, her seat was occupied by Sofia, so she went to sit next to the photographer, who asked what she did. You know, said Julienne. Nothing. There was quiet till the food arrived. Leïla slurred to the table, We're so lonely in London; the only person who has introduced us to anyone is Gaspar Tehrani. Do you know Gaspar Tehrani? Today Gaspar Tehrani wrote me, You should meet this person who is awesome, but also this other person who is really awesome. (They all felt badly for the other Gaspar, who had just secured a tenure-track job in archaeology at Princeton, because no one was in archaeology at Princeton.) Julienne dripped a bit of oil on her napkinned lap and considered using a knife to cut her pasta but worried that everyone would laugh. The Oxonian was an architectural historian of Aleppo hoping to complete a manuscript on urban interventions under the French mandate and was concerned about securing a visa. Axel scoffed that she knew nothing; this was just the beginning. The masseuse announced that his scarf was from a flea market in Damascus, then wriggled his chair to excuse himself. The rotation of his elbow knocked over Julienne's wine glass, which immediately atomized. Some boys at a nearby table clapped and whistled. Julienne got up to squat above the sanguine pool to pick up the larger pieces and drop her napkin to absorb the liquid. The wine had gone to her head and she lost what was left of the glass.

E♭

You wouldn't believe me, but I'm not angry with you anymore. Years after your death, you live deep in the marrow. As such, you who are dead are simply life, and I, living, am a parasite. When you talked about ending your life—and you had, so often—it felt as if you were naming a possibility and, as such, that it could not happen. We had learned together in life that nothing ever materializes in the way one imagines. So when you discussed methods and materials, I was not quite comforted but knew they could be eliminated if you realized the concept in full. I thought that you had found a different way to die, into another person. You did so many things I never could have imagined. You, who warmed to the sun, moved to a cold and peaceful country that shone its warm gaze on you for hour after hour in summertime, then stole it all away. When you finally married, you chose a singer whose lungs could nourish all the atmosphere, who emits the whole light of the midnight sun or another cliché of serenity about blonde women who would not snap like an icicle if asked to hold your pain. I am told, repeatedly, that she is the daughter of a famous architectural theorist. While I still don't understand the joke, I can imagine her father and yours mourning you in every place, dearer friends than they might otherwise have been. I think all the time of what you chose to do with your life and what you did with your death. You and your mother, she who had mastered the proof, surely fought about the matter. Who were you to play the gods? Your choice defied her, logic, your son, anyone who dared to love you. Who massacres himself, in the way that you did; in the way that you told me you would so that I could ensure that you wouldn't? I still half expect you to emerge from somewhere. Maybe you became a hermit, high on a hill in the far north. It would be enough for me. I think, especially these days, of what might happen if I could count out my days on fingers, with pebbles, in grain. Did you have that sense of inevitability? Or were you also shocked by the ways in which you fell through the ice?

F

Dr. Sarkarov had a soft accent, from both Queens and the former Soviet state in which she was likely to have been born—eventually Julienne discovered that this was Azerbaijan—and her office was cold in temperature and decor: chevron-patterned floors stained in light gray, an LC4 chaise longue for the patient and a Barcelona chair for herself, both in white leather. On the glass E1027 table was a manuscript by Melanie Klein reprinted in the original as a single thin volume to look like sheet music. Julienne liked her straightaway because she was not afraid of trying too hard. She steeped lime-flower tea and did not offer Julienne any. Without asking anything of her life in the present day or what had brought her to this stark room, Dr. Sarkarov asked questions that Julienne nearly refused to answer—whether she had been sexually assaulted before the age of twelve or whether she had an abortion—and declared that Julienne tended to absorb the texture of the things that had happened to her and molded herself to the expectations of others. Am I wrong? asked Dr. Sarkarov. You have allowed yourself to take different shapes, to parent yourself in ill-equipped ways, as if you did not have the tools to raise yourself. Suddenly the room seemed very ugly; the wall of windows looked into an air shaft redeemed only by the coo of pigeons.

G

She had been working on a series of castings—inanimate, lifeless objects—mostly to reteach herself the medium and materials. Sometimes she felt a bit embarrassed by what she was doing, cowering over her work like a rodent so that no one could see it. She would, for example, pour a soft polyurethane casting rubber over an old key— today the one to the door from the last apartment she shared with Gaspar—and afterward cut the slab laterally in half so that there was a life-size section model of the object itself extracted like the pit from a stone fruit, but clean, with no hanging flesh. That was all; that was the work. From the corner of her eye, she watched an older woman with a nose ring throwing small pots, spilling the detritus of art making all around the table on which she was working, listening to something with a twang that exceeded the capacity of her headphones, which might have been a classical raga or Dolly Parton. Julienne was fascinated by women prone to slovenliness: imagine taking up the space that might belong to so many others, like liquid, drowning one's way through life. She had, nevertheless, something in common with her: neither of them was really making art. At least Julienne wasn't, she thought after examination of her tiny, bouncy echo chambers.

A

Willa worked long days in Newark and, having to drive more than one hour each way, was not usually able to collect Julienne from the ballet school or whichever free activity the local community center offered in the afternoon: painting, some kind of science class, karate taught by a nerdy high school kid whom she had watched try and fail to slash a plank several times. In the worst of weather she would ask a friend's mother for a ride, but otherwise she would—literally—jog home. The distance was only three miles, but for most of the school year the sun would set as or well before she was dismissed. She had little homework in grade school (or could finish before the day was done) and was relatively unencumbered by her backpack. She was free: old enough to know that what she was doing was undignified but young enough to pass off the backpack running as a coach-ordered activity. Julienne was admirably fast but not freakishly so—if the fastest two girls were cheetahs, she aspired to the gazelle—and joined the cross-country team. She enjoyed those runs and the discipline they brought to her life, but her very favorite ones were solitary, early mornings in spring, summer, or early fall when she could see the slightest tickle of light on the horizon bleed into a full day. Her soles held their own power. She enjoyed discovering bouncy qualities in every surface and in the elements, running against wind, rain, and snow. She went as hot as a vapor, springing from every surface, but this only sweetened the cool breeze that rewarded her. As she got older, she would run against traffic on the highway or through thinly trodden forest. For her, learning to drive would scarcely signify liberty, but whenever she felt compressed by life and the pain that accompanied it, these freedoms were the sensations—the ones she could never really get back— for which she wished most in the world.

LIME SCALE

B ◌

Julienne's new favorite beverage was whole sweet limes in water, warm or cold, with salt or with honey. The ritual made her feel a bit Victorian, although she had picked up the habit from her housemates in Berlin, who pointed out that they were probably destroying their enamel, but it didn't really stop them. This was the case with many of her college-acquired habits, like her proclivity for black clothing, which friends insisted looked ideal with her coloring, which only intensified during her stay in Berlin, which brought about ridicule from her mother—like

Julienne's new nickname, Morticia—of whom she saw less and less, the busier she became with school and with work; this year she debated not going home at all during winter break. Some of this reasoning was financial: unlike her classmates' parents, Willa had no yoke over her; the College had given her a full scholarship that included a small loan and something called work-study, which meant that earnings from the library or cafeteria might be applied automatically to her fees. She was able altogether to eliminate these obligations by traveling to Cleveland twice a month to work as a catalog model. A recruiter, stalking the bus station at which Julienne had arrived the first year carrying four suitcases, had given her a card; she worked for a large catalog business that had many subsidiaries. Just beautiful, she had said, snapping Julienne's exhausted blank stare as she fought not to inhale all the exhaust. At eighteen, Julienne had smooth and even features, all planes, no shadows, every tooth, eyelash, and pore small and where it should be; she fit all the sample sizes and could model one T-shirt every twelve seconds, peeling off the garment and pulling on a new one in a different color without wrecking her hair.

She held telephones in different shapes. She was delighted by different bicycles. She worked diligently from airplane seats. Every shoot took place indoors against a plain background; much later she would find photographs of herself in a forest, on the beach, après-ski. That summer she did not have much time to work: the previous school year in Berlin ended one week before the start of the new one at home, but she booked shoots every week in September, left to her own devices in writing a thesis on Joseph Beuys. On Labor Day (which she found ironic, having spent the day working), the shuttle bus back to campus was very crowded. Normally Julienne chose the aisle seat behind the driver and stuffed the window with her belongings, but today she had only a small handbag with fruit salad and *Ways of Seeing* in it. Someone banged at the glass door, a gangly geek who made prayer hands when the bus broke hard. The doors opened. The geek apologized for his luggage. The grumbling bus driver disembarked to open the storage from beneath the vehicle. Julienne looked around and realized that the window seat next to her was the only one available and moved over. The guy got on the bus and flopped down next to her—men were so terrible at sitting down and getting up, she thought—as the bus sped away, earlier than the schedule promised, which gladdened her even if she had to sit next to someone so lanky his knees wouldn't quite fit, the cage of his limbs threatening her space. He kept looking at her and turning away, listening to a cassette player to which he hummed very quietly. She put in earplugs and removed the fruit salad—mango, banana, and pineapple bathed in lime—which she ate very slowly as if doing so would blunt the sound.

C ♯

Leïla's thirtieth birthday party was held on the rooftop of the Peninsula. The plan had first been the Indian Consulate, then the French Consulate, then the Consulate of Ecuador, but the party planner could not reconcile non-negotiable choices of decor with security. Julienne was impressed to see that ice reproductions of sculptures by famous woman artists had survived the journey, including a colorful Niki de Saint Phalle and a delicate Barbara Hepworth. It was stunning work, especially for the end of

July. They sent a comfortable chill into the air. Gaspar was doing a residency in Banff with a string quartet—all day he would send her pictures of perfect mirrored lakes and God-cut mountains. Julienne arrived at half past ten, regretting her decision to wear a long white dress on the subway no less; she had liked the flow of the fabric but now felt dowdy and formal among women dressed to dance. Men seemed to descend on her and each time she sent one away to buy a drink another would arrive; she wondered about these guys, walking around ham-fisted looking for her, condensation spilling through their fingers. The other Gaspar approached with something verdant. Don't worry, he said. I took care of them. Thanks, said Julienne mockingly as she accepted the platonic essence of pandan leaf. You ruined my experiment. The other Gaspar said, You just don't seem like a funny girl—it's always a surprise. Julienne said, I really should have asked you to sip this first. Who knows its contents? The other Gaspar said, I watched the bartender. Never mind, said Julienne. The other Gaspar said, You really are going. She said, Then tell me a sad story. Come on, he said. I don't like to laugh too much, she said. Okay, said the other Gaspar.

My aunt tried to poison me when I first came to Denmark. I was five years old. What? Julienne recoiled. I stayed with her for a month while my parents were still working in Ethiopia, the other Gaspar said. The famine was long. My adoption had just been finalized. They didn't want to risk taking me with them. My aunt was angry that they had brought me home and said she wished I had been a gypsy instead, or a wild animal, all in the same maligned category, of course. It wasn't very subtle: there were pills and liniments by the stove. I quickly learned not to eat what she gave me and to sneak a glass of milk in the middle of the night so as not to starve. There was a dog in the neighborhood whom I loved. I don't know to whom he belonged if anyone. Of course I couldn't feed him anything from her house. She rarely said anything about my lack of appetite. It turned out that she was feeding him, this starving dog, the dinners I hadn't eaten, and he died. I know only because she told me afterward, glowering. That's terrible, said Julienne. I thought I had seen him starve to death, the other Gaspar continued, but—forgive me—the signs were not the same. What a monster, said Julienne. Your parents must have been livid. No, said the other Gaspar. I didn't tell them anything for years, till after she took her own life. They felt badly for her, and by then, I did too: a broken person stewing in her own poisons, with nowhere to go. She sounds like a wretched and hateful person, said Julienne. She must have been glad to go. No, said the other Gaspar. None of us are very far from misery. I don't believe in bad people: if you endure enough venom and abuse, you may think that you know the shape of it, that you might spare others such a fate. But if it doesn't stop then slowly everything in the body is replaced every seven years and there is nothing left but hatred. In a way she cannot be blamed at all. The other Gaspar looked quickly at his watch. I'm sorry, he said. This is the cake time.

D ♩

Julienne had left Gaspar's parents' house on Boxing Day, alone, driving the rental car back to the Bronx: she could no longer abide the presence of Axel and Leïla in the tension after Gaspar's return from Turkey; events in Homs were escalating and Gaspar would not tear himself away from the news. The next evening they spoke on the phone for forty-five minutes and decided to separate. He had remained in Connecticut but would come over to pack while she was at work. He had agreed to stop by on the second Sunday evening of the new year to move out the last of his things and to settle the bills. So she decided to turn over a new leaf and cook dinner. Something simple yet nourishing, nothing that seemed fussy or try-hard. She had usually made breakfasts and he had usually made dinner. Willa had warned her not to cook for a man or he would think of her as a mother. Not Sana, of course. Still, eleven years in, she had cooked an evening meal for them both perhaps twenty times. Their neighborhood grocery store sold all kinds of rot at twice the price for those deemed undeserving of vegetables. She walked across town to Fairway in bitter winds. Suddenly she remembered one of her favorite winter dishes from Germany: liver dumpling soup, with a side of red cabbage and apples, and maybe a cucumber salad. She found a Spätburgunder from Baden in the wine shop and took a taxi home. She scrubbed every inch of the home, cleaning around Gaspar's packed things—he should, after all, remain free to come and go—returning the place to its prelife shine and the sunny day on which they first visited when every day seemed like the flower-lined alley out the window and the bells of an unseen church. She began to prepare the dumplings: soak bread; roast onions in melted calf's kidney fat, then let them cool; mince together the liver, fat, soaked bread, then let everything sit for half an hour whilst she cubed cucumbers for the salad and nicked her finger on the dull blade—it made her want to call off the whole occasion, which could have been handled through the postal service and a moving company. When Gaspar arrived, he rang the buzzer although he did not have to, and then the bell. She put the cabbage on the stove before she answered the door. He seemed fragile, all bones, as if he would crack if he fell; his skin was pale and clammy; he reminded her of an abandoned kitten. From habit she tried to kiss him hello. He turned away, like a small child, and buried his face in her shoulder. She gave him a final squeeze and, trying to radiate equanimity, instructed him to sit at the dining table. I made dinner, Julienne said. It's almost done. It's awfully early, Gaspar said. But I skipped lunch. Were you able to find a place for the truck? Julienne asked. Andreas is coming with it later, Gaspar said. I told him we needed to talk. Good, said Julienne, smiling. She offered him wine in the massive Spätburgunder glass she must unconsciously have purchased for this occasion. He said that's enough to a thumb's worth. You know, I felt strange about coming here, Gaspar said. But I'm really glad I did. Good, Julienne said, smiling again. She took out the dumplings from the refrigerator and brought beef stock to a boil. Is something burning? he asked. Julienne pinched herself to keep from cursing. The cabbage and apple were burnt and stuck to the skillet. One fewer thing to worry about, she tried to joke. She removed the dish from the stove, then opened a window and turned on the fan. How were the rest of your holidays? she shouted over the noise. I can't hear you, he said. She dropped in the dumplings and tried to concentrate on the tureen but everything stank.

E ❧

You hadn't shown up in my dream life for months. Yesterday I dreamed that I ran into you with Andreas, your protector, someone I never learned how to be, of whom I was always jealous. We were all at a concert, in a friend-of-a-friend jazz composer's apartment on the Upper East Side. When the two of you left together between sets, having spotted me in the crowd, I chased you without my coat or shoes into the subway station, the 2/3, so that I recognized it as a dream. You had no blood left and were pale, cold, and thin, like milk. I grabbed your arm and demanded, Why do you still hate me? You ranted and raved about many things that couldn't possibly be true, like that I had gotten you fired from your job and that I had no right to call my sister who worked in finance boring because I was the boring one, but I don't have a sister. You shouted, And she's still boring!

F

Bob had never been to the home she shared with two twenty-seven-year-old Barnard graduates that sat atop the Pacific Avenue entrance to the Atlantic Terminal, mostly because it had blue-violet youth hostel walls that seemed to derive from a phthalate. They did not socialize

with any of the other's friends. Bob would take long weekends away, to the beach with friends, or the woods with
friends or—once—to the desert with friends on a trip to
Marfa with colleagues. Julienne remarked that this was
a strange choice for corporate tax lawyers, but Bob had
shrugged and said that some of them liked art: he did,
after all. He seemed always to be on business in Boston—
a lingering issue with the Big Dig that had been revived
again and again for the previous decade—or visiting
family in Duluth. He'd lost an uncle recently to an overdose and his mother and cousins were not only inconsolable
but needed legal advice. His father lived on the opposite
side of Minnesota, near Fargo, and was on Bob's second
avaricious stepmother, which, he said, had given him
unpaid and unsolicited experience in family law. This
unavailability had catalyzed the collapse of his marriage
to Heike, a hedge fund manager who looked like Julienne's
childhood idol Katarina Witt, and who—he confirmed—
had been a youth figure skating champion in the GDR.
She had never been so jealous. He and Julienne spent
most of their time drinking wine (she admired his

extensive collection of appropriate glassware) and watching old movies. His apartment in Red Hook was filled with more timber than Julienne had thought legal under local code. There was a wood shop in the neighborhood, but he had converted the dining room into one as well; he had built most of the tables and shelving in his home. The latter were filled with volumes of French literature and history, which he had studied before law school, as well as historical carpentry manuals. This eccentricity consoled her, she told Dr. Sarkarov. As such she confessed that Heike's presence hadn't upset her nearly as much as she expected. Dr. Sarkarov said, You would like to be with someone without wondering where he could be, who he was with, what he was thinking, whether he was thinking of you and whether he would return someday. Someday? Julienne repeated. You know that he exists in the world, said Dr. Sarkarov, but some of the appeal is that you do not know when the last words will be. Julienne thought about this. He looked like a bear in the glow of the streetlight but like a werewolf in the daytime in his lumberjack clothing that he sometimes even wore to work and none of it mattered because they never could belong to one another.

G ₄

On what turned out to be the anniversary of Gaspar's death, Julienne joined a ceramics studio in Sunset Park. The floor and brick walls were washed starkly and tiled in white, there were long blond tables and sliding corrugated screens to divide the room into seemingly endless permutations bathed in natural light. There were bright jars of natural pigments. She had also looked at a private, walled space with extremely high ceilings that must once have housed freight or fighter planes. But the ceramics studio was a place so beautiful that it moved her, that she might no longer fear the company of others. The office manager smiled when she handed Julienne the keys, as if they were a secret. She found a table in the back of the room near a long window. She filled a lamp with violet methanol and lit the wick, which warmed her face in the January cold and thawed the knots in her throat and chest, and after heating her knife took fine slices of wax to mash in alternate hands so not to burn herself. She curled the material around an almond. She cut it open when it cooled and looked at its bath-pruned-thumb imprint. Perhaps it was enough for her to be in a studio, a ceramics studio of all things, when she had taken one ceramics class ever, having thrown away her studies on acrid resins; maybe the throwing away of money at a problem was enough. Suddenly she grew hot. Gaspar had really been gone from the world for a whole year and something he'd said was correct: the failures of aspiring artists turned them into cultural benefactors—despite her strictly limited means she spent money on this hob-byist playroom, museums, galleries, art supply stores, the federal government, so many banks changing hands like a folk dance and the for-profit art school that owned her debt despite having launched many fruitful careers that could not be hers; her generosity was contingent on her never having succeeded. But what good was talent if it meant winding up like Gaspar, whose mathematics of the undead had buried him in the boreal forest? Suddenly she wanted to drink the hot lamp alcohol: one of her mother's hippie friends used gentian violet as a natural remedy but

Salers Gentiane, the aperitif, was yellow. Instead she reheated the burnisher and carved in the waxed almonds a pair of large dark eyes and long sharp nose and big, big mouth. She kneaded away the soft form in her palms till it disappeared and held her fist over her chest.

A ♮

Julienne and Willa went to Montana at the start of August, just before Julienne started college. On the journey she alternated between reading *A Lover's Discourse*—from the list of books most loved by students sent by the admissions office—and a biography of Camille Claudel. Willa was cooing over a novel; Julienne couldn't make out the fluffy script in shiny, raised lettering unlikely to help a blind person, but there were large, bared pectorals on the cover, also raised. They had a layover in Denver (Willa's career allowed them into the airline lounge) and as mother and daughter enjoyed, respectively, a tequila sunrise and a chamomile tea, Julienne considered that they were preoccupied with the same questions: (a) What was it to master someone else's language; and (b) How consciously did one decide to throw away one's life on another person? Often this relationship was not romantic: Claudel's thirty-year institutionalization and mass burial seemed to have happened under the thumb of her reactionary poet brother rather than Rodin, no saint. Sculpture was a kind of compulsion for Claudel; it was not so crazy to imagine a sculptor tenderizing clayey Provençal limestone in her palms absent her usual materials behind the backs of nurses and orderlies. Grandma Judith met them at the airport in Bozeman. She congratulated Julienne on being the first woman in their family to go to college. What are you studying? she asked. I hope it's business. The school doesn't have a business major, said Julienne. What kind of a school is that? asked Judith. They have economics, said Julienne. Maybe you'll do something for this economy, said Willa. It's that Hillary's fault, always nosing her way in; Bubba should have stayed single. No, said Julienne, the Thai baht disconnected itself from the US dollar. But what? asked Judith, confused. At four in the morning the next day, Judith took them fly fishing—a two-hour U-turn toward Bozeman—pointing out the landmarks with which Julienne had become familiar over the years: the old Anaconda Copper Company smelter stack and the Berkeley Pit in Butte, which they could not quite see, an eruption of geologic gorgeousness that she could not quite reconcile with her mother. Judith and Willa were nearly master anglers, wading in for the catch. Rowing saps your strength, explained Judith. Julienne hated using worms as bait so used the commercially produced ones her grandmother bought just for her. Judith caught the first rainbow trout of the day and Willa a whitefish. Although the sun had not yet shown its head, Julienne was hot and went to sit on a tarp they'd set up at the riverbank. She was so sleepy. She scraped together some of the loam and began passing it back and forth between her palms, pressing out the water. It was fun to use harvested earth as a material; sure, it was disgusting to have watched her classmates play with mud in grade school, but adobe buildings and such were still standing, so perhaps there was something to it? She molded bits into a person, into flowers, into fish. She woke up to the genetically piercing cackles of her mother and grandmother. Are you making mud pies?

Judith crowed. You wouldn't even do that as a child. Willa, get the camera. Quick!

B ◌

Julienne was gifted with the ability to sleep through anything. When she felt a tap on the shoulder, she presumed it was the driver announcing their arrival, but it was of course the towering nerd next to her with a question: Excuse me, he said in a tone so overly polite that he could not seem to decide whether to use words, do you know whether the bus lets off at the Conservatory? She was irritated; literally anyone awake could have answered the question, especially the driver seated directly in front of him, but she said yes. Right. Are you just arriving for the term? he asked. No, Julienne said. I had an appointment in Cleveland. Right, he said. Oh no! Are you like sick or something? Julienne said, That's none of your business. He was ruining her favorite part of the journey, even if being on the left side of the bus meant not being able to see the soft blue horizon of Lake Erie. Right, he said. Are you a student? She said, Yes. It's my final year. There was something about his face, the way he held his mouth open, the way he repeated the word *right* like an eighties banker that she found annoying, but there was something else about him, a kindness; maybe he really did want to be sure she was okay. He said that he was on a yearlong fellowship at the Conservatory in music composition and performance and had just returned to the States from Aleppo, where he had been studying the oud for the previous two years. Despite wanting to make him feel badly, Julienne terribly enjoyed the German lute (and the zither) and, genuinely interested in this piece of information, asked whether he had been studying it for a long time. He said that he hadn't but had studied classical guitar for many years, and having played in a jazz band on a cruise ship for a whole year after college decided to study instruments one could never bring on such journeys. But they're so small, said Julienne. What a nice way to fall asleep on a boat. No, he said, people don't like to be challenged musically after a certain age. We were advised to play the greatest hits from exactly thirty-five years earlier to meet the youth of the average traveler. Early Beatles.

Beach Boys. Elvis. Our choices, not terrible. Julienne asked his name. He said it was Gaspar. Julienne asked, After the friendly ghost but in French? He said, Touché. No, after the myth and some music. What's yours? Julienne told him and he laughed. Were your parents fans of the Marquis de Sade; Juliette plus Justine? Gross, said Julienne. No, my mother just liked it, like the matchstick vegetable. Were you at least born in July? he asked. Not even, she said. So do you cut vegetables in Cleveland? he asked. Are you a chef? Julienne said, No. I was working, though. Gaspar said, You seem to have a tedious and expensive commute—are you like a tax lawyer? Not really, said Julienne. Gaspar said, Now I have to know. Julienne said, after a deep breath, that she worked as a catalog model; that very hot day, she had to try on a hundred turtlenecks and pose with heavy metal office furniture. Wow, said Gaspar. So you can model literally anything. Like for painters but also like those huge plastic dolls in shop windows and agricultural equipment? It's a real range of ridiculous products, said Julienne. I never find out what they are till the images are published. Gaspar said, Wait, taking out a gently gnawed Bic from his pocket and putting it behind his ear, squinting slightly. Do you think I could do it? The few graduate students on campus were mildly creepy, as if they couldn't survive among adults. But there was something disarming about Gaspar, who wasn't hideous, with nice eyes and a great deal of hair; the tiny sprinkle of acne on his chin didn't repulse her but instead hinted at a bit of excitability, as if something in his skin couldn't wait. She giggled suddenly. What? he asked. I also posed with a singing large-mouthed bass, said Julienne. It plays classic rock songs about rivers. They both laughed. When they reached the campus, he asked her to his apartment that evening. When—although not quite sure this was true after her year abroad— Julienne said that she had a boyfriend, he gave a dismissive wave and said, Going to a grad student's house for herbal tea and a medieval string quartet is highly unlikely to present a threat. Bring him, he said. The more the merrier.

HEMOGLOBIN SCALE

D

The days were lengthening. She had not heard from Gaspar in weeks, which turned to months. The office was unofficially closed from Good Friday through Easter Monday, but Julienne was obligated to manage the telephone even though Jürgen was in Germany and everything had been redirected to his cell; she received sales calls from novices wanting to talk with Dzurrgunn Waggoner or the person in charge of procurement. All day long she threw the I Ching: will Gaspar return my calls? (48.2.3 to 8: Yes, but it will be unpleasant.) Will Gaspar show up at the apartment without warning despite having left the keys on the kitchen table? (22.3.5 to 42: Yes.) Will he come back for good? (22.3 to 27: Yes.) Will I tell him to go away? (53.2.5 to 18: No, but good fortune anyway.) She had written him pragmatic things about the utilities, silly articles from magazines he loathed, lengthy explanations of their last conversations. Until the separation they had not gone more than two days without speaking. A week earlier Leïla had been in town from London and had presumed, despite Gaspar's absence, that she could stay in the spare bedroom now, absent all his musical equipment. She had been polite to announce her arrival but had never actually asked Julienne, who did not want to seem petty or, worse, rude in asking why Leïla could not stay in the copious abode at the Apthorp, owned by her family, where she had dwelled for the previous decade. She, who often saw Gaspar during the day, spent the visit altogether refusing to discuss the situation. Instead she took an interest in Julienne's future: Would she try out something new at work, perhaps in the arts; was she planning to take a roommate once the lease ran out since she wouldn't be able to afford the apartment on her own; was it difficult to dissolve a nonmarital domestic partnership and how similar was it to a French PACS; was she dating anyone and who was it; if not, did she spend her evenings spinning thread? After she left, Julienne threw Leïla's sheets—smelling of garlic, neroli, no shame—into a trash bag to quarantine them from the rest of the laundry, then hoovered, mopped, and opened all the windows. The spare room felt emptier now than when they had moved in. Gaspar had moved the storage locker from the room but beforehand courteously placed her old materials into a box, untouched for years: dry plasteline, a cracked watercolor palette, a large sheet of acetate chalky at the edges from which a rough square had been removed (his doing, with scissors). She sliced an inch from the plasteline with a proper knife and kneaded it with her right hand, then her left, passing it back and forth, pressing it between her palms. It went soft; despite the biting cold of her fingertips, this reminded her that she had warmth to give. She pulled the material thin and wrapped it around her thumb then pulled it off in one go. From some impetus, a modern person evolved sufficiently to ingest synthetics like a novel Soylent Green, she popped it into her mouth and bit down. Examining the dental impression, she was pleased with herself: Julienne, who had never needed braces and brushed carefully after every meal and snack, still had perfect teeth. She had mentioned to Gaspar that she had kept, in one of her jewelry boxes, a film canister of not only her baby teeth—there were ten; Willa had found them repulsive but her grandmother had begged her not to chuck them and now Julienne was stuck—but all four of her long, ugly wisdom teeth taken out in one go; Gaspar had taken her home afterward and testified to the weirdness of her words: if it was strange to keep one's old teeth, it was strange also to discard them. She shook them all out into her palm. The baby ones were upsetting. The wisdom teeth reminded her that she was unwise. She should give them to Gaspar. She wanted nothing. She should give everything to Gaspar.

E

Your pain ended so that ours could begin. I refuse to know how you did it, although a part of me wants to. Dignity says do not ask, love says that I hope you are no longer in pain, concern says that I hope the finder of your body cared for you. I will never know whether you walked farther and farther into a sheet of ice till it could no longer bear your weight, whether you put a hole in the ground and drank yourself to death in the boreal forest, whether you in the hallucination of freezing to death used the last of your energy to stumble up to a peak and become a hermit. These are the gentlest things I can imagine. All day and every night, I try to know. It is an antiseptic wish: you thought that I would make a good surgeon. I took it as an insult, but maybe it wasn't; maybe you thought, for a while, that I could put you together. I can neither imagine you of this world or outside of it. You live in the layer wrapped loosely around the planet, but it is heavy. It is the weight, the compression, the anchor left behind for the living.

F ♯

She had not been invited to the funeral, but there was a wake at Gaspar's parents' home in Connecticut. The invitation had come by email from Gaspar's Norwegian wife, Mina. Julienne felt duty-bound to go, although she would not really be welcome there and did not want to. His wife and son would be there, and his parents, and those he considered to be friends. She felt foolish, standing on the cold platform at Grand Central early Sunday morning in the dumpy black garments that were once her nice clothes. The carriage was mostly empty. She sat at the edge of the punctured vinyl bench. The train galumphed along but she found herself grasping the seat as if to slow it down. Something about the shaking of the carriage made her hurt. Each jolt pummeled her. There was no rustling in the world sufficiently anodyne. Gaspar had hated this journey; they would instead rent a car in the Bronx and drive the rest of the way. When the correct stop arrived, Julienne looked around at the carriage. There were more passengers than she remembered. She couldn't recognize any of them but it was January and everyone was covered up in many layers of clothing. Descending the stairs to the parking lot, she felt heavy. There was nowhere to sit. Julienne knew that Gaspar's house was not within reasonable walking distance of the station. She put the address into her phone: six hours and nineteen minutes' walking; thirty minutes' Uber. The wake would not start for another hour. Across the road she saw the shadow of a pond. She went down a side street, past another parking lot and some kind of radial community center, then slipped promptly upon toeing the hard, lightly icy ground. Her formerly dress boots clung to nothing. There was no path from where she was to the water and she went from tree to tree to maintain her balance. The bark snagged her gloves, so she took them off; seconds later her hands were frozen mangled. She looked all around her. There were hints of light and water and noise but she was lost. How far could she have gone? She tripped over a sticky, ropy root and planted her face hard in the ground. When she lifted her head there was a dot of blood in the snow.

G

She planned to spend four days in Hong Kong and ten on the mainland. The crowds at the airport gate surprised her, with so many infants, disoriented by the time of day—it was past midnight at JFK—and this cold, alien place on an ordinary Wednesday. This would be her first trip outside the United States in years, the first ever outside Europe. The first to Asia; the first without Gaspar: Where had her life gone? She boarded the plane, which would catapult her over the North Pole: her mother had warned her about all the radiation (many times that of an X-ray; pilots and flight attendants at her airline were permitted polar routes only thrice a year), so Julienne had booked a return through San Francisco, even though she didn't mind. This was her last thought before falling asleep on the plane, rather unsoundly; it was colder than hell, even in winter clothing burrowed into the window. The babies, on different time zones, harmonized a fifteen-hour choral piece that she could hear despite earphones and the critically acclaimed blockbuster to which she could not pay attention. She switched to the map; they were now over the Northwest Territories, labeled in their original language. Out the window the clouds broke and all she could see was blue water. Long ago, Gaspar had told her about a dream he had when they were sitting by a lake that was choppy and welcoming at once. Julienne, he had said, was coaxing him to go in. I kept pleading that I would drown. A flight attendant asked about eggs or congee. She asked for a whiskey: Who knew what time it was? Her next awakening was due to the pressure of descent and she gasped first at being jolted and then—most unexpected—at her surroundings: steam, cliffs, volcanoes. She did not have a vocabulary word (and could not construct one in German; she'd gone rusty) to communicate this simultaneous feeling of deep peace and fluttery excitement. It was just after five in the morning when she reached the hotel. She showered and fell asleep at seven to a familiar symphony of bleating horns. The next time, to her immediate horror, she saw the digital clock it read 23:02. Privately mortified and also starving, she hound-bounded outside. It was raining, and so quiet: all she saw was the stillness of the harbor in the fog and the glimmering glass shore. She wound up at the rooftop bar of the hotel next door and asked to sit by the window, where she gazed at the melon-egg just below her line of sight. The kitchen was closed but the staff found her olives and nuts to accompany the tea she ordered, generosities she never would have expected in New York. They were so nice, she thought; if she had been born in the city of her conception would she be a colleague of

theirs? Around her were tables of Australian businessmen plying each other jovially and lawlessly; there
weren't that many of them in the world compared to
other businessmen, so how did they wind up everywhere?
Uncharitably, it struck her that all the most recognizable
buildings in the skyline were banks. Gazing over the
harbor, she reasoned that even if (as Dr. Sarkarov had
proposed) Willa's story was nonsense, it did not necessarily mean that there was not some truth to it. Maybe
her biological father had a modest job with the municipal
government and lived in one of the many tower blocks in
the city. Maybe he was an American flight attendant whose
memory embarrassed Willa or some other American she
wanted to forget. Maybe he was from Hong Kong but
Indian, or maybe he was just a bad guy.

A

Julienne won a prize for drawing at the end of ninth
grade. With the exception of her teacher, no one congratulated her; instead they said, Of course you did: every
girl who won the drawing prize for the previous three

years has been Asian. She asked one of the Indian boys what they meant by that. He said, It's like when I won the times tables contest. Everyone in my kathak dancing class knows how to quickly multiply sixty-seven by thirty-three; it's a surprisingly useful skill. But I can't spell, so . . . he shrugged. They only know I'm Chinese because I've been telling them so since kindergarten, she said. She confessed to him that she was angry but not sure why, a sentiment aggravated after she also won the geometry prize, previously earned by the same Malaysian girl who won the drawing prize two years earlier. Walking home alone that afternoon, she began to wonder whether winning prizes for drawing and geometry meant that she was good at those things. After all, prizes had to go to someone. If she was good, where could her ability have come from? Willa indicated no aptitude for drawing or geometry—Julienne's logic could not rule out the possibility—but perhaps it came from her father, the surgeon: the tenuous connection she had to people and a place she had never known. At home she rearranged the dining table so that she could organize her school supplies and put them away for summer. It wasn't her fault that she thought about where things should go and how they should be, she fumed silently. And did those qualities—not so far from the secretarial skills for which she would later deride herself—have anything to do with talent for the things she liked and which interested her and seemed to point to higher things than organizing her school supplies, which, again, she rather enjoyed? No matter: she began to count the paper clips that she kept in an empty Altoids tin. After her mother came home in the evening, Julienne asked her to tell the story again: the whole thing. The best way to glean information from Willa, she knew, was to imply that her life was unusually thrilling; although she now worked as an executive assistant and not a flight attendant she still received free flight vouchers, not that she would ever give any to Julienne. Willa said: I signed up for flight attendant interviews as soon as I turned eighteen. They were recruiting from all over America and I was supposed to start in Seattle after the training in St. Louis, but they based me in New York. Fresh off the bus from Montana, I catapulted to Denver that night. Just a year in, I got the biggest prize: first class from New York to Los Angeles to Hong Kong and then Sydney! Not bad for a girl who had never been on a plane before taking the job. I was one of the most successful stewardesses there; I'd been to Atlanta, London, Dallas, Paris, Detroit, Rome, but never the Far East. Back then we landed at Kai Tak Airport—it's closed now; the landing was extremely dangerous, right over the city. But anyway, at the lounge in LA I noticed the most handsome man. Do you remember that sexy communist opera movie you made me rent last weekend? He looked like that guy. He was wearing a beautiful blue suit—you had to wear a suit in first class those days unless you were a rock star; everyone did—and was drinking a martini, reading the *Herald Tribune*. Inflight I offered him champagne, caviar, cigars, funny local foods—although for a while all the cuisine was Polynesian no matter where in the world we were going—and he said no thank you to all that. We locked eyes for ten seconds. He didn't seem the kind for staring, so I knew it was a come-on. Anyway, just before deregulation the airline industry was a party: drugs, huge bottles of booze, exciting knives, flowers!

Four kitchens. The whole upper floor was a gorgeous cocktail lounge, with the best bartender I've ever known. Our uniforms were chic and sexy too, none of that frumpy gray polyester you see now. No flat beds of course, or—ha ha! Anyway, I paid him lots of attention. We were allowed to sit and talk with the passengers back then. He was a doctor, a surgeon, not one of those wimpy doctors. But I also played coy. Only when I fastened his seatbelt before landing did I leave a silk scarf with my perfume on his shoulder. (Here Julienne expressed that she would have been very displeased if someone left a fragrant rag on her shoulder.) Upon landing, I escorted him to his car. He took my hand and pulled me in, with my stewardess suitcase. We didn't leave the hotel room till I took off for Sydney two days later, but we did watch *Hiroshima Mon Amour*. The characters were He and She, Hiroshima and Nevers. So we decided not to introduce ourselves. He said, You will know me as Hong Kong, and I will know you as Anaconda. Julienne was very confused; the story sounded like something out of Willa's *Cosmopolitan* magazines, whose lack of negative space had always annoyed her.

B♭

We can make it a day trip, Julienne had insisted to Gaspar before they boarded the train in Hoboken, on a Saturday morning in May. My mother's house is very small. Gaspar had said that he didn't mind and quipped, Do you know what kind of places I've slept in? I got stuck in the supply closet on the cruise boat and simply passed out from the fumes. No one opened it again till five in the morning, whatever time zone that was. I also hitched from Aleppo to Damascus in an empty livestock cart. It was a long drive and I'd already read my book, so . . . Julienne laughed politely, hiding her hurt at this comparison. After they arrived in Hackettstown (twenty minutes away from Julienne's childhood home) she gave a call alerting their presence. They were settled on the station steps with yogurt and the crossword when Willa arrived one hour later. With hardly a hello she lunged to hug Gaspar, cooing over his great human height. She offered him the front seat of the fuchsia Ford Fiesta she was leasing. Julienne braced herself for the spontaneous end of Willa's hospitality, which came when Gaspar said, It's so funny that we're between Oxford and Vienna. Willa asked, Why? What should towns be named; are you from the Shangri-La or something? Mom, said Julienne, it's just funny that places are named after other places. Relax. Willa shouted, Funny how? The car went silent. As provocation or otherwise, Willa pointed out important places: the new Starbucks, Wawa, Mount No More, and the names of loosely incorporated townships: Cornish, Foul Rift, Hazen, Little York, Manunka Chunk (later Julienne and Gaspar agreed that name would make an excellent ice cream flavor), and Buttzville. Julienne squeezed Gaspar's elbow as if to restrain him. They went for lunch at a Mexican restaurant with good margarita specials. There Julienne slowly sipped from a glass that was mostly ice and quietly shuffled away the car keys from Willa's consigned pink Prada handbag, relieved that Gaspar did not ask whether the chef could make him a huitlacoche porridge and that her mother had ordered only one pitcher of watermelon margarita, which Gaspar thankfully did not call a jug. Willa asked, So what do you do again, honey? Gaspar said, I'm doing a doctorate in music composition. A doctorette? Willa repeated.

Like a little doctor? Julienne said, It's a degree. It's the most advanced degree in music. So what, do you hammer knees? asked Willa. Or ears—what do music doctors do? Gaspar said, It's like a PhD but with a creative dissertation. Willa said, It sounds like unemployment to me. Gaspar laughed and said, Doesn't it? When he excused himself to the bathroom, Willa scoffed. I don't like him, Julie—he's smug. Julienne balked. He's being very nice, she said. You're not making it easy. Well, I have a sixth sense, said Willa, reapplying something shimmery on her lips in a pocket mirror, and some of that fiberglass insulation is still in your head.

C

Gaspar took an extra semester to finish his DMA in Aleppo. There had been plans for Julienne to visit. I've told my old host family about you nonstop, he said. This time he lived on his own in New Aleppo but saw them often. The couple were Karim, a craftsman who made and restored wooden doors, and Fariha, a literature teacher who had gently but rigorously perfected Gaspar's written grammar during his first stay. Their children were nearly grown, the elder at the University. Gaspar was not so fond of his modern building: it's weird taking an elevator home, he'd said. On the way in he often stopped in a café; he had become friendly with the proprietors, who were also musicians. The ones at the University were not divas, he explained. I'm sure there are bigheads in the department, he said, but I've only met the thoughtful and devoted. Gaspar studied oud and classical Arabic music theory; he also taught piano and composition to undergraduates. The students, too, he said, were very good. Few of them had sufficient access to a piano for regular practice, but their eyes and ears were sharp: They just get things, he said. Gaspar usually finished in the early afternoon and either went home to compose—it was important not to forget the rush of sounds and thoughts that came each day—or for a long walk. There were hot planar surfaces left behind by the French at the center of the city on the way to Ancient Aleppo. Gaspar would sometimes join the handful of modern office workers eating shawarma in the square; at others he would sit for a bit in the tessellated courtyard of Umayyad Mosque, which had the most extraordinary minaret and a mihrab with splendorous polychrome, he said. It had been restored recently and had a garden to the north, under which a new library had been built. Also, John the Baptist's dad is buried there, he said. In case he likes to read. If Gaspar had dinner plans with his host family he would stop in the souk for fruits, nuts, dates, pastry, whatever looked good. The vendors recognized him from his previous stays in Aleppo, the last ten years earlier; recently one had told him that his aunt had seen Gaspar purchase a cantaloupe. The family prepared simple dinners—some mezze, usually a kibbeh, something sweet at the end with tea—and their lives were not lacking in adventure or amusement. The youngest, for instance, was in a play and was learning swordfighting moves. Something I could help him with, said Gaspar. After dinner there was always music, with the family—Karim himself played oud and would lend Gaspar a drum, then they'd trade off—or with other musicians in the city. The scene here is amazing, he said. So many young composers, instrumentalists, singers, chamber groups, bands. Just unreal. He began to play riqq and tabla in an ensemble with nay, oud, zither, and violin. It isn't difficult to create music here, he said. Every sound goes together just so: the din of metalworkers, the swell of motorcycles, the call to prayer. It's the best moment of the day when they converge. Julienne asked tentatively: Why don't you try to spend more time there? You sound so happy. Gaspar said, Well, it is a fascist dictatorship, after all. There's an election, but opposition parties are banned, so Assad will win again. I can't keep up with my meds here, which could be banned eventually from the country. By the way, did you know that nightshades can trigger depression? There's so much eggplant and tomato in the cuisine. And I don't want my parents to have visa problems when they visit. The situation is so volatile. But there are places that feel like poetry to me, that call like home. I wish I could stay here forever.

D

The next day, Holy Tuesday, Julienne went to the art supply store down the avenue and purchased UltraCal 30 Gypsum Cement. From a drugstore she obtained insulin syringes, vacuum tubes for blood collection, gauze, alcohol, tape, and gelatin capsules. Needles did not scare Julienne: in college she had donated her own eggs to couples wanting tall, attractive, more-or-less white children, stabbing herself in the stomach with hormones every day for two weeks. She cleaned the whole bathroom carefully with bleach, threw down clean drop cloths, and then filled exactly one syringe with blood. She took a second one to ensure that there would be enough for the gelatin capsules, which she filled without spillage. On the stove she melted carnauba wax—urethane rubber would have been better, she realized later—and brushed it in layers over Gaspar's old loaf tin, which had been of miserable quality, so he had decided it should be hers. She mixed the UltraCal 30 Gypsum Cement in a disposable aluminum foil pan and poured in a single layer over the wax once it was solid. She then laid in the teeth and blood-filled gelatin capsules, which she reasoned would float in the cement and eventually dissolve; then, after fitting a meter of vacuum tube, she reinjected it with the spare syringe of blood before pouring in the second layer. It would not take long to cure. On Wednesday night she went to see *Jiro Dreams of Sushi* with her friend Jennifer from college. On Thursday morning she spritzed the construction with water. On Friday morning she released the object from the pan and scraped away the wax with steel wool. It was imperfect but pleasing: the tube, being open-ended, had let the blood into the concrete without spilling it all over the place. Some of the gelatin capsules had dissolved, permitting the blood to come to the surface like blueberries in pancakes. She could see only one of the teeth, but that was ok: more haunting still would be the implication of teeth. Through the weekend she felt much better. On Monday she purchased a roll of bubble wrap and the smallest box to comfortably fit the material. On Tuesday she shipped it—two hundred dollars, with insurance and a declaration of hazardous contents— to Gaspar's attention at their first home together, his parents' pied-à-terre.

WATER SCALE

C

Gaspar had been invited to score a film in Turkey—
something to do with Xenophon's *Anabasis*—and would
be on sabbatical from LA, Thanksgiving through the following summer. He seemed to gleam with an orderly,
healthful Southern California sunshine, doing tai chi and
laughing yoga every morning, dragging her to Mysore
sessions and macrobiotic dinners out when they were not
noshing on robust bowls of miso soup with the delicate
Japanese vegetables of land and sea he had sought out in
midtown on the counsel of a chef whom he had befriended

in Venice. Julienne did not understand Angeleno and imagined seaweeds and kabocha squash boiling in a nonna's pot with the laundry, all to be pinned and drained over the canal as a singing gondolier rowed by. They went to meditation sessions at zendos throughout the city, an ashram upstate, a Hindu temple in Queens designed by a holy architect from Chennai and yoga studios led by sinewy teenagers delivering moral lectures as they led the class through happy baby. Thanksgiving with Ali and Sana was, for perhaps the first time, entirely nice: they seemed to miss Gaspar and therefore all that accompanied him. The weekend weather was unseasonably pleasant; they spent time on the wide porch or in the gazebo, talking and drinking wine or tea and playing board games. The annual retrieval of the Christmas tree was not at all fraught. Gaspar would, on Tuesday, leave for two weeks in Turkey, with the director and producer. Much of the film would be shot in a two-thousand-year-old amphitheater near Antalya. They were being a bit cagey, said Gaspar. I worry that there might not be a film at all but a collection of gladiators, or just a tiger. I should read Xenophon. They returned home late Sunday night. It was still warm out. There were bits of discarded turkey and bone on the stair that formed the trail of an undead pied piper compelling vultures to the roof.

D ♭

The days were inching brighter by the second and she couldn't sleep past perhaps four thirty. Julienne would prepare coffee but could rarely keep it down unless she added a splash of rum to it. She had never been much of a morning drinker, but this was the only way she had found to quiet herself, and after all, Gaspar must have gifted her the leftover alcohol on the way out for precisely this reason. She rarely deliberately went to bed, which, weeks later, still smelled of the coumarin, terpenes, sulfates/sulfites/scrambled egg, benzene, and fleur de sel that made up his scent no matter how frequently she bleached the pillows and the mattress pad. Every night she crumpled as if it were the first time, toothmossed and mascara-crunched, onto the secondhand sofa from their second apartment, which, without the Mongolian blanket Gaspar had reclaimed, was salt-and-pepper polyester dandruff; she had thrown something over it but the knowledge made her squirm. Diminutives felt odd in her mouth, so she had never called Gaspar by the simplest of cozy terms except as jokes in the earliest days, often in German, but chunking carrots, in her first attempt at cooking since the liver dumplings, knocked her to the kitchen floor when she sliced off a square millimeter of skin from her fingertip, which she wrapped in a tea towel, then two. Pet sounds fell out of her mouth in rolls; maybe this was merely the soft keloid of an ancient wound, a tenth-great-aunt or uncle hacked to pieces in a tenth-great-grandmother's arms by a tenth-great-grandfather, and while she knew that, however privately, this thought meant she was nothing more than a bigot ignorant of the history of the Western Hemisphere and the carrots would rot and mold, over the week.

C

It would remain warm. The next day Julienne woke up too early. She did not look at the time till she was on the train. Afterward she could not stomach going into the office and purchased a coffee to sit in Zuccotti Park. It felt so small without the tents from Occupy Wall Street, bare trees tangled with delicate bulbs, granite benches popping out from the ground like tendons. In the office most of the MDs were in Frankfurt and Zurich, brokering the last of the year's deals. The atrocious baby bankers dumped heaps of sticky receipts for her to enter into the system. She kept disposable face masks, hand sanitizer, and a box of latex gloves for precisely this purpose. All day she punched in numbers, cheerfully declining their requests to be reimbursed for magazines, alcohol, and unauthorized first-class travel. She sent a text to Gaspar asking how his own travel preparations were going and heard nothing from him all day despite other texts asking after the packing. He had a lot of prescriptions, she thought. Did Turkey require any vaccines? No, she caught herself. She tried calling him and heard nothing. He was so careless; maybe he left his phone home. When she returned home the door to their apartment was ajar. Gaspar? she called out. She poked her head into the dark room in which they normally worked.

Everything appeared to have been overturned, knocked every which way, wires and papers and clips everywhere. She picked up a heavy metal curtain rod leaning against the large storage cabinet and tiptoed down the hall, past the bathroom, still soggy, fan blaring, into the kitchen, watching out for the no-kill mousetraps and dry bits of cracker they held within. She looked over the counter into the messy living room, blankets everywhere that she had not noticed in the morning, which indicated that he might have spent the day in a fort. She knocked softly on the bedroom door in case he was sleeping, or worse. Gaspar? She knocked again. She then held her breath and opened the door. It was pitch-dark. The blinds were drawn. The bed was unmade. This had been a habit of his to which she had never become accustomed; were there not the imminent risk of being murdered, she might have taken a split second to pull over the duvet; how long did it take? She shut the door and went to peek in the spare bedroom, open, bright, untouched. She heard the angry shuffle of the front doorknob and gasped. Then a pounding against the hollowed steel as if a hole might be borne and as if she might only see the battered fist, battering ram, batter bat, when it came through.

E♭

Objectively speaking, my life would have gone better without you. How dare you put such ideas in my head? Not of the great artist, for which I would need that ineffable quality, that combination of gall, arrogance, and solipsism. I speak of the well-educated little woman, surrendered to your every need, the sort of mother you might have wondered about as a child, who absorbs poisons to turn them inward. You molded me from compression and in tension, like an anchor. This is why you did not want to go into the water. In dying you transferred your pain unequally throughout the fiefdom you left behind. It isn't fair, but as surely as injuring my nose branded me as your own, my debts from graduate school today total more than one hundred and forty-three thousand dollars, although I only borrowed eighty. I have been paying them consistently for twelve years, but only the minimum for eight. You finished your doctorate and began to depend on me for health insurance. Then you left, then I lost my job at the bank, and then you died, and then I took a poorly paid job, and then I got sick, and then I stopped caring: because what is a future? You didn't want one. Sometimes I will read about men who call themselves futurists without irony, software engineers, management consultants, and advertising executives who do not know that the poet and artist Filippo Marinetti formed the Futurist Political Party, which was absorbed into the Fascist Party. Or do they? Did you? Your indelible brand, in my flesh. You might say that you are blameless, that I was still young, but my debts are multiplying as fast as anything else in my body, as large as the loud hollows you left behind, time in infinite dimensions. When I open the house-sized slender envelopes, I see not only my debt to a bank, but to you: tithing to the church of your life. I know that you are there because I wanted to make a home of you and made one instead of debt. What are you hitting me for? You would protest. You would say that you did the math and sacrificed your life so that I could be released from your shackles. But these are not our choices.

C

She froze. She thought about going down the fire escape, so shoddy, with the flimsy drop-down ladders that rattled in traffic. The bell rang: surely no criminal would do something as pedestrian as that? I'm home, Julienne shouted. I'm opening the door. Please. She tiptoed to the door and peered out the peephole: it was Gaspar. What the hell are you doing? she demanded. Why did you shut the door? he asked. Because I thought we were being robbed, she said. Please let me in, said Gaspar. I'm sorry. Julienne unlocked the dead bolt and took a deep breath before turning the knob. She turned away from him and walked down the hall. I'm sorry, he said. I was moving some things to the basement; I'll need more space if I'm working from home. But why did you leave the door open? Julienne asked. You have pockets for keys and don't know any of our neighbors. Whose fault is that? Gaspar demanded. Stop, said Julienne. Just don't do it again, all right? I'm sorry, Gaspar said again. But I'm done. Can we order some food? You choose, said Julienne. I can't keep track of your diet. That is, if anything you can eat delivers all the way up here. That's just racist, said Gaspar. No, said Julienne. I pay your health insurance when you cross state lines, so order something that won't make you sick. She stopped herself, breathed deeply, and affected a relaxed smile. Listen, she said. You'll be away for a whole month. Order whatever you want; I'll open some wine. Do you need help? No, he said. Only I know where things are. There are materials and equipment that I need to organize. Then I have to edit some work to show the producers. Okay, said Julienne. I understand. Gaspar sighed. Sorry. Thank you. Is Japanese all right? Of course, said Julienne.

F

The bitter chill woke her long before the sun came out. She wondered about the heat. She put on thicker socks and a sweater, but they were not enough, so she wore a hat and fell asleep till the wool stretched over her eyes. Hypnopompic, she opened the news on her phone. There was a breaking story: the offices of *Charlie Hebdo* in Paris had been attacked; several of its staff had been murdered. She did not understand this at first; instead she had believed *Charlie Hebdo* to have published something offensive about a shooting. She would have had no familiarity with *Charlie Hebdo* were it not for the boyfriend of a roommate in Berlin who would leave out the most graphic of each issue's cartoons splayed at the kitchen table. It seemed like an absurd choice for a shooting: who would kill the staff of *Mad* magazine? Then she saw a message from the other Gaspar that said, I'm so sorry, but in the twilight of her sleep she imagined that the first Gaspar—her Gaspar, if she could call him that in her mind still—was saying as much but not to her; he was apologizing to grass in a field on a hot day. She was watching him from the top of a hill and knew not to disturb him; she was no longer a part of something private. It was still dark when she began to get ready for work. When she returned from the shower she checked her phone again. There indeed was a message from the other Gaspar that said I'm so sorry. What was this; had he drunk-texted her from somewhere in the Pacific? If so, she would call to wake him up and he would never do it again. The other Gaspar picked up on the first ring. Hello, he said a bit more flatly than usual. Hi, said Julienne. I got a text from you—are you all right? Oh, said the other Gaspar. Not really. It's really terrible news. You mean the shooting in Paris? Julienne asked. What shooting in Paris? asked the other Gaspar. I haven't seen the news today. As you can imagine, it's been a bit much. What's going on? asked Julienne. I wanted to ask how you were doing, said the other Gaspar. Fine, I suppose, she said. It's been a long time. The other Gaspar breathed in and said, I need to ask you a very stupid question. All right, said Julienne. Did you know that something happened to Gaspar? he asked. No, she said. What happened? Well, he went missing for some days, he said, and was found quite far away. He hadn't taken anything with him; he left his phone and keys and passport and medications at home. Mina was worried about that at first. She thought he might have been kidnapped, but . . . Is he okay? Julienne asked. Uh, no, said the other Gaspar. He was found on the west coast. California, she said. No, of Norway, said the other Gaspar. Among the fjords; it is very mountainous, in a thick boreal forest. He had purchased a ticket in cash but the police were able to detect his face from the cameras in the station and there was a search for him. It was in the news there. But is he okay? repeated Julienne. No, said the other Gaspar, a bit more firmly. He died. For some reason Julienne felt a bit giddy, as if she were up very high, as if she were about to be dropped. She lay down; her pillow had gone very cold. No, she said. No, no, no. I'm sorry, the other Gaspar said again. I feel as if I am always delivering you the worst of circumstances. No, she said. I'm just shocked. Did he get lost hiking? He paused. Hello? Julienne said. I don't know, said the other Gaspar. They haven't yet done the abduction. So he was kidnapped, she said. No, he said. I mean the examination after someone is dead. I'm sorry, she said. But it feels like a bad dream and as if I might sleep again and he will be alive and well in Norway. I'm so sorry; I just found out from Mina's sister and texted you straight-away, he said. She's taking care of Aram and the calls and everything. It's a mess. A Rahm? Julienne asked. Like the arrangements. The other Gaspar paused again. No, he said. Aram is Gaspar's baby. You didn't know. Of course you didn't. Jesus. I'm so sorry. It was only then that tears reached Julienne's eyes, but they did not feel real; she could not trust the motives of her ducts.

C

It had occurred to her to tidy up, but she instead went into the bedroom for an ill-advised evening nap and wondered if she could convince herself to stop waking up so early. Her dream had foxes in it. Gaspar was rapping quietly on the hollow door. As she came to, he went in and knelt next to the bed. He kissed her forehead and said hello. Are you all right? he asked. Long day, she said. Food's here, he said. I got you that miso eggplant. Thanks, said Julienne. That's so thoughtful. He had set the table with long plates and big spoons and chopsticks. He had also made a cucumber salad with a chiffonade of shiso leaves and plated the rest of the food beautifully. There were candles. Where did the sake come from? she asked. You've been asleep for three hours, said Gaspar. Oh, she said. Have you finished packing? No, he said. I needed a break. I wanted to see you before everything goes to pieces in the morning. Do you want me to take you to the airport? She asked. No, it's JFK, he said. Well out of your way. Save your days off for Christmas. I really wish you could come with me; you'd love Turkey. Julienne said, My neighbors in Berlin were all Turkish; I think I told you. You did, he said. Now just imagine them without state-ordered discrimination. I just couldn't, said Julienne, smiling tightly. What are they like?

G

Backpacking after Berlin and before the Eurozone, Julienne had slept in airports and stayed awake in train stations, toting from city to city in tourist map cocoons one small bottle of infused olive oil—smoked wood from Seville, basil from Genoa—to flavor breads purchased in slurries of pfennigs and centesimos and pesetas. Fifteen years later she was pleased to find that jet lag was still her favorite altered state: the twelve-hour layover on the way home from Hong Kong had left her enough time to gaze at San Francisco in cliffs and fog—addicted to cliffs, she was—while reveling in the company of a whole burrata for lunch with oregano flowers and squash blossoms. She then spent the afternoon in the rose garden at Golden Gate Park beaming daftly at every rumpled velvet head cocked toward the sun, followed by the Pierre Bonnard exhibition at the de Young, although the star of the museum was, once again, the view. Her feet hurt from two weeks of gallivanting and she wound up in a large bookshop armchair with an iced hojicha and stacks of fragrant travel magazines. She was growing sleepy and decided to purchase a paperback for the red-eye home. She chose the memoir of a poet laureate who had recently lost her husband, a painter whose work graced the cover. They had a whole life together, a real one, with nearly grown children; as he evaporated from his body she saw him in transit. One of Julienne's real tears blunted the print. What a nice book, she thought. I should buy it. Just then a voice from the rear left of her own brain shouted, That's not what happened! It slapped the book from her

hot red hand and kicked her sharply, in the spine, out
of the shop.

C

You know that isn't what I'm saying, said Gaspar. I mean
the loss of culture, history, architecture; the sense of a
world that is different, or which could have been, or one
that will be different, soon enough. Imagine being unbur-
dened of that loss. You've just described anything, said
Julienne. He sighed and continued, Turkey mediates—
and is frequently exploited for the ends of—many
supranational families, like the EU, or groups of Islamic
nations or the efforts of the US and its allies to destabi-
lize the wider region. It shares a thousand-kilometer
border with Syria and has already taken in eight thousand
refugees. Julienne said, Is that bad? Gaspar said, No. Of
course not. Just . . . as the American Empire continues
to decline, the energy from the Arab Spring felt very
promising, but now hope is being diminished because
there's no logical end to all this. So what are your plans,

when you get there? Julienne asked. Gaspar said, I'll arrive in the evening, so we'll probably go to dinner and not talk about work. I worry, though, that I'll have nothing to eat. Today I got all of these B vitamin shots and the guy at REI showed me this survival gel—I bought sixty packets. Come on, she said. He said, wheat, dairy, nightshades, eggs: it's a minefield. Julienne said, I never thought you would use the word minefield in that way. Sorry, he said. Won't you miss out on the local cuisine? she asked. Aren't there grilled vegetables and meat? Yeah, he said, but there are so many eggplants, tomatoes, potatoes; they're so poisonous. You should quit them, too. Well, if Turkey successfully manages to carry out the American experiment, there might be substantial quantities of survival gel for us all in the near future, she said.

A

Busy at work through the week, Willa would record her favorite soap operas and watch them with girlfriends on Saturday afternoons. Julienne would return from ballet class or soccer practice to find them suffocating in laughter at the bereft heroines. But I'm your wife, one of them would whine mockingly in a nasal falsetto. That's why I'll break every bone in your face, growled Willa in a deep southern accent, and they would all die cackling, splashing themselves in iced white zinfandel as she tip-toed into her bedroom. Your brat is like Houdini, she overheard one of the women say. She also found her mother's boyfriends to be odious: always drunk, going after Julienne the second she turned perhaps twelve years old, and the worse they were the more likely they were to move in. Sometimes they would stare at her not necessarily from desire but what appeared to be confusion. Your mother says you're Chinese, said Rick. Are you from there? Hank often asked her for advice not only about Willa but about women in general. It's difficult to maintain a relationship once a woman turns thirty. A woman's cycle is anchored to the moon; every February when the Lunar New Year restarts and the anointed animal changes, a whole year of woman births falls off a cliff. Cliff stayed for three years and nearly married Willa. Once he had tried to hit her with a belt; Willa had grown up not on a farm but in proximity to many of them and used her scouting skill with twine to make sure that he could not get up. Then Julienne called the police. He had tried again to propose after that, turning up with a bouquet of polyester velvet red roses, asking Julienne on bended knee to be his daughter. By then Willa had someone new as well as a sizable collection of firearms—she promised to take Julienne for lessons as soon as she was old enough—but managed to chase away Cliff with some gardening tools that had gone hitherto unused.

C

Changing the subject, Julienne asked, Have you had time to work on the piece? No, said Gaspar. Because I wanted to spend time with you. Well, thanks, she said. I'm so happy that you're here. He said, I wasn't sure whether to spend the sabbatical in New York. It's not the best place for me to write. Oh really? she asked. Well, how about you? he asked. How's work? Fine, she said. Nothing of interest to report. Are you still following that German guy? Yes, Gaspar, said Julienne. My boss for the previous seven years. Dieter? he asked. Jürgen, she said. You've met him half a dozen times. Are you still moving between floors? he asked. Sometimes, she said. Phone coverage. Like the executive floor? he asked. You know, she said, New York has things going for it that Syria doesn't. Sure, he said. But I'm going to Turkey. She continued, You have a community of musicians, colleagues, libraries, studios dating to high school. Our families are nearby. Your whole adult musical life has been based here. More the reason to take exile, said Gaspar. And Syria? Julienne demanded. What about Syria? he asked. Do you think I'm going to Syria? I wouldn't be allowed to enter the country. Maybe you ought to sneak in, said Julienne. Hitch. It's where your soul is trapped. Find meaning, right? That is the cure and not your four hundred medications. She dropped the dishes vertically into the kitchen sink, mildly disappointed that nothing broke. Gaspar sat at the table with head in hands, massaging his third eye with his thumbs. Is there something you want to say? he asked. Yes, she reasoned; the cruelest thought she ever had about Gaspar, so cold that it shocked her: I hate your mediocrity. Instead she said, Why can't you stay in Turkey? Or go somewhere else, even back to LA, which has its own Venice? Or—why not—Syria? They must need you there, the one place on Earth where you don't feel small: and you should! Her face felt stiff. She wanted to cry but nothing seemed to emerge. Instead she shouted, You are an arrogant dilettante whose life is every bit as inconsequential as mine. Do you know how small you are?

B♭

It took them till Halloween to get together, but only till Halloween. Julienne did not want to suggest that he had worn her down, but she had stopped finding him (prohibitively) strange only recently. It turned out that Gaspar was, indeed, to some, including Julienne's girlfriends, cool, and cleaned up well with a haircut, and the patch of acne disappeared thanks to a cream sent to him by his mother. There were many contradictions; he was a reasonable dancer and had been a three-sport varsity athlete in high school (to be fair, chess and fencing had been among them) but would trip in the sidewalk. Sometimes I just fall, he explained. He was very good at combining fruits or vegetables with herbs or spices but also spent days working on a composition with a different passionate intensity, leaving the studio only to retrieve vending machine food. He truly seemed interested in Julienne: her background, he insisted, was much more interesting than his: her family were from Montana, as exciting and beautiful a terrain as Mars, and her mother and grandmother were independent and adventurous like she was. And half her heritage, he said, was a seductive wild card. He was interested in her life, her work, her friends, her stories; he wanted to know her favorite sounds, smells, colors, with not a whit of prying or competitiveness. He lived in a sunny studio half a mile from campus. Most of the objects in the room had cost him little or nothing but were utterly irreplaceable: small wooden instruments, tapestries woven by his host family in Aleppo, framed paintings from artists in different cities around the world. Everything fit neatly in boxes and suitcases when they needed to, ready for his next home. One night he had kissed her on the way home from a party—dressed, like five other girls, like Charlotte Rampling in *The Night Porter*—with the perfect balance of surety and clumsiness; they didn't leave his apartment for days. (Well, just two consecutively: Julienne had an exam in The Contemporary German Novel and had written an impassioned three-blue-book essay in her very compact second language on *The Emigrants* that, despite the excessive length, received an A-plus.) Most of the boys she had dated had drained and demanded her attention, siphoning away something of herself, searching for their own reflections in her eyes. She liked the person she was with Gaspar. Her school work was better, sure, and she was happy but also friendlier (Jennifer's science-major friends were no longer scared of her) and funnier (she had recently told a whole joke). Was it selfish to love one's reflection in someone else? she mused. Maybe it didn't matter. She was in love.

C

Gaspar, bewildered, seemed to avoid her gaze. I need to get back to work, he said. Let me load the dishwasher. I'll do it, said Julienne. Then I'll come and help you. You can't help me! he said. Can we please let it go for now? We won't have time to talk tomorrow, she said. I'm not disappearing into the jungle, he said. We'll talk tomorrow night, at worst. How can you say that? she demanded. We're not going to resolve this tonight, Julienne! he shouted back. I have to work. It was then that she began to cry. He so rarely shouted in front of her. Come here, he said, embracing her. I'm sorry. Me too, she said. I don't know what's wrong with me today. Well, time to do the dishes, she said, breaking from his grasp and sad, puppy-ish eyes. Eventually he went back into the study. She only heard rustling. He must have been wearing headphones. She finished the dishes, brushed her teeth, washed and rubbed unguents on her face, changed the sheets, made the bed, and fell asleep. When she woke up in the morning—at half past five—she expected that Gaspar had fallen asleep working but couldn't find him anywhere. She called his mobile and got his voice mail. She texted, Are you OK? Maybe he had something to do beforehand; but what, possibly? She sent a note to Jürgen and the secretaries who covered her phone saying that she had a small family emergency and might be late. At seven (the time at which she normally arrived at work), she saw a text. Taking off, wrote Gaspar. Bye.

IRON SCALE

D

The admin who covered Julienne's phones at lunchtime
had failed to tell her that a dinner in Berlin with the
Federal Minister for Economic Cooperation and Development had been postponed to the following evening.
Jürgen, experiencing an existential crisis over having
been stood up by his own nation, had not been permitted
through security. Julienne had spent the whole afternoon calling every federal office she could locate and the
cell phones of every admin she knew in the Berlin office,
but no one answered after hours. Jürgen had stopped

returning her calls; he might have gone for a currywurst. At the end of the day she was conducting her ordinary desk sanitizing routine when a group of the girls passed. Hallo! Julienne chirped as if they hadn't seen each other all day. In German, she asked, Do any of you know about Jürgen's dinner? Yes, said one of them, the most senior after the office manager. I phoned and alerted him to the change as well as his staff in Berlin and made alternate reservations for him and his wife. Did you add it to his calendar? Julienne asked, furrowing her brow. The other assistant said, I don't have access and he does not trouble himself with such administrative obligations. That is your job. Bye-bye, she added in English. On the way to the subway, Julienne purchased a bottle of wine; she was going to Jennifer's to make pizza at her new apartment in Bed-Stuy. On the train, she read Gaspar's review of a book written by a composer who taught at the same college as his mother, whom he seemed to have known personally and whose music he had played for Julienne (which she found creepy); the book, named after an introductory music course he'd taught, took the lay reader through a hundred canonical works of experimental composition, their very form and genealogy—there was a gorgeous image from John Cage's "Cartridge Music"—and she was bemused to read (a) that Gaspar found the work potentially intriguing even to the milquetoast office drone in search of a new hobby, and (b) that he likened the youthful exploration of music to the exploration of new corporeal adventures that one might find coura-geously at any time in life. Gross, she thought. How much sex was he having these days? Or, on reflection, not hav-ing: was this repression? She shuddered at imagining Gaspar at, like, an *Eyes Wide Shut* party all gangly in a robe and went completely off him for at least the rest of the day.

E

We had discussed marriage with some continuousness, in a logical and diplomatic manner. I had said that I didn't want to burden you. My debt from graduate school likely exceeds the current market value of my mother's house and the 1984 material cost of your parents'. If something were to go wrong, neither you nor your line of work were very stable, and your family is comfortable but there are unlikely to be any secret oil fields. I descend from strong Germanic women, teenage single mothers from Montana reared on country ballads who gave me all the warnings against marriage. For this reason, I always found the gamble dangerous and romantic, one's whole life in the other's hands. After all, did same-sex couples fight for nothing, and do they flip a coin to decide who is owner and who is property? Years later, I can see that you were trying to protect me from you. Instead you chose someone who could weather such a loss, someone less brittle and cold, which took you to Norway. When I met Mina for the first time at your wake, she exchanged my dry handshake then pulled me close to her. She saw that my clothes were damp and that I had a cut on my face. I understood everything, I think, not about why you tethered to her, but why you truly loved each other. Maybe she saw you in a way that I could not, because we were too young. Your son, Aram, wasn't there, but she asked if I wanted to see a photograph of him and I said, Yes, please. She did not know how crushed I had been to see him. He had dark blond hair and gray eyes. His face looked nothing like yours, despite your abundance of strong features. Maybe this means that he will become just like you were. He was nearly four decades younger than me, but I read him, another fatherless child, as a brother.

F ♯

Bob suggested a July weekend in the Catskills at a cottage he liked very much; the TripAdvisor link sent Julienne down a rabbit hole that led her to discover that he had spent Memorial Day weekend there with Heike, who gave the house five stars with special praise for the earth oven, which they had used to make a stew of locally sourced squab with stone fruits. He had told Julienne that weekend that he was suffering through a document review. In response to Bob's invitation, Julienne sent a text that read, No, thank you, and refused his calls. She read the review out loud to Dr. Sarkarov that week, who had responded, Well, that's it, then. What's it? Julienne asked. Dr. Sarkarov said, You replied, no thank you. That is very important: you measured what he had to offer and refused with as much grace as you should muster. Julienne asked, Shouldn't I talk to him? No, said Dr. Sarkarov. Men are given substantial slack in our society. Do not make excuses for his deception or lack of imagination—did you say that his ex-wife is named Heike? Yeah, said Julienne. She was a junior East German figure skating champion and is now a managing director at some weird British hedge fund in New York. So she's loaded, said Dr. Sarkarov, but that's not my question: Why are you so obsessed with Germany? Oh, said Julienne, her face warming. I wouldn't call it obsession. Okay, Dr. Sarkarov said coldly. Berlin was always in the news when I was growing up. The wall fell when I was about ten years old. I was curious, but my high school didn't teach German. So I took it up in college. It seemed like a culture able to face its own ghastliness. Have you ever tried to learn any other languages? Dr. Sarkarov asked. No, said Julienne. I fear losing it now that I no longer speak German at work all day long. Faulty logic. When Gaspar was alive—here Julienne bristled—did you ever try to learn a language that he spoke? asked Dr. Sarkarov. No, said Julienne. He learned

Farsi from his father and his mother taught him Arabic but was only really fluent in the latter, which is to say that it was a family thing and I was not invited. I know a little Farsi, said Dr. Sarkarov. We studied it in school. What about music, were you close to his work? Not really, said Julienne. And now the thought of listening to anything he wrote is unbearable to me. I'm wary of trying to reconstruct him. Okay, back to you, said Dr. Sarkarov. Did you ever study Chinese, to understand that side of yourself? I really thought that I would, said Julienne. It's a visual language, which intrigued me but was also intimidating, so far from English. That reminds me, said Dr. Sarkarov. Your parents' meeting story is extremely strange. They were strangers, said Julienne. I can't be the only patient you've had who never knew her father. Consider this, said Dr. Sarkarov. Your mother was a flight attendant: Could she not have read the passengers' names, in an airplane silly enough to include a piano bar? They got rid of the piano bar before then, said Julienne. Fine, said Dr. Sarkarov, but would she not have tried to rummage through his belongings while he was in the shower. For god's sake, said Julienne. My mother is many things but was not going to rob him. Besides, her name was Anaconda and his was Hong Kong—why spoil the illusion? Dr. Sarkarov asked, What film did they see again? *Breathless*. No, *Hiroshima Mon Amour*, said Julienne, exasperated. Did you ever check to see whether *Hiroshima Mon Amour* was available to watch in Hong Kong the year before you were born? How would I find that out? Julienne asked. Dr. Sarkarov shrugged. If you were really motivated you could trace the distribution of the film, but what would change for you, she asked, if the story were different? Julienne said, my mother always told me that my father was a surgeon in Hong Kong and that I could find him when I grew up, like my schoolmates who were adopted. Till then, I had only her. I would look in the mirror for hours at a time, for something. Looking in the mirror seems important to you, said Dr. Sarkarov. Julienne bristled again. But what if your genetics—even your mother's—didn't matter as much as you seem to think they do? Julienne rolled her eyes. I have nothing in common with my mother and am clearly not white. Dr. Sarkarov shrugged again. I wouldn't say that. You look just like the girls I grew up with, the tall, pale, pretty girls with a Russian parent or grandparent. You could be anyone.

G

Her forehead and spine ached almost continuously and every morning she woke up hacking as if her throat had been stuffed with fine, sharp feathers, but she had been to urgent care twice and both strep cultures came back negative. Sometimes the down from her jacket or old duvet would dust her sweaters; maybe she had inhaled them, maybe she was developing allergies in her ripening age. Sometimes she considered everything she had breathed in her lifetime and wondered whether it was city life, the fifty cigarettes she had smoked in her lifetime mostly before the age of twenty-one in bucolic Ohio, or maybe she was simply allergic to her new office job at an arts center, which despite its noble mission and free classes was quite boring and miserably paid. Every day she considered Bob's offer to move in with him: I want us both to be protected, he had said. Even if she were liable for half the mortgage and co-op fees and bills and—if she'd heard him right—property tax, even if he wanted to arrange a real lease dictating that he owned the dwelling with terms of damage and eviction included and her current monthly rent would increase by one hundred and fifty dollars every month to extend her commute by at least thirty minutes and she would have not a thing to herself, not a room and no furniture, it would mean a witness or even an alibi; the knowledge that she was quietly dying in front of him would make him culpable.

A ♭

Julienne couldn't remember much of the incident, but it was a favorite story of both her mother and grandmother. She was about three: Grandma Judith, visiting from Montana, was repairing the insulation in the attic after the failure of the handyman Willa had hired, who had also covered the floor, walls, and countertops of the bathroom in tile but left behind the cheap bathtub enclosure, ignoring the black mold that oozed from beneath the slap. In short, the place was a wreck. An ordinary, just-hidden stair led to the attic, which storybooks had told her would be a magical place. She marveled at the pink clouds and went to play in them. She was in short order coated in a strawberry rash of fine cuts which made her itch, but they didn't stop her from mashing the beautiful substance into her mouth, lashing her tongue and cheeks. They did not take her immediately to the emergency room but tried instead to induce vomiting. Julienne, wailing from pain and confusion, could not understand her failure. It was then that "Eye of the Tiger" began to play on the radio: What did it mean; had Julienne found a force within her that would allow her to fight against the suffering and humiliation or was it just an awful song? No matter: Willa's favorite part of the incident was that Julienne had been foolish enough to eat the insulation. Judith's favorite part of the story was that Julienne's skin turned the same shade as the material. Julienne's favorite part was that they considered this incident to be worthy of retelling.

B

Julienne was giddy the night before the first day of classes and even giggled spontaneously as she struggled to go to sleep. She would have her own studio! As an under-graduate she took studio classes but as an art history major worked in the rooms where the classes were taught and had to shelve her work when finished. All first-year students had been registered for the same courses, explained the program's coordinator, who was a profes-sor of painting. Julienne was surprised by the talkiness of the schedule in front of her: Colloquium, Criticism, Semi-nar, and Practice. This is not an avocation, warned the coordinator. I recommend strongly that you rearrange all aspects of your life, whether they be social, material, environmental, or otherwise, to meet the expectations of the program or suffer duly. Afterward, Julienne sat in a room with her fellow sculptors and their advisor, Jack, who had a show on view that he encouraged the students to see. But if you ask me about it, he said, you're out of the program. Julienne was younger than most of the cohort but not the very youngest; she had neither the gumption of the skateboarding teenager who asked about network-ing or the single mother of three whose last child had just started college and measured the passing of time and money in taps of the foot. Well, go on, said Jack. Your first crit is on Thursday. Get to work! On what? Julienne thought. They hadn't been given anything to do; their classes hadn't yet begun. Julienne went to find her studio space, three ten-by-ten OSB panels painted white and a good place to go insane. She wished that she had a door so that she could lie down on the concrete floor, heart pounding, and ask what she had been afraid to: What—if anything—did she have to say? It needn't be anything grandiose, she reckoned, but would have to be more than enjoyable. Beuys, after all, believed that everyone alive was obligated to engage creatively with the world, that anyone could make art: sculpture had a social purpose. He had nearly died in a plane crash, saved only by Tartars who wrapped him in felt and fat to keep warm. His art, Julienne thought, was of the body. Her art, she decided, would be out of the body. She chose a metalworking elective and a time-based media course, which she worried would force her to design robots. She thought that the seminar class would be easy for her—she had been a good student and used to debates spinning out the door—but was not prepared for every discussion to become a personal critique of an opinion's expressor, distilled through the lens of what the accuser imagined they were. Working in acetates and resins, welding metal and wielding wire, she saw that one did not necessarily begin a project with a thesis, outlined like so many art history papers, but by thinking through material, using it to see. Her first project in time-based media was a short video of a walk along the West Side Highway rendered through a fiberglass resin flower cast in bronze that she used to direct the light. Is this a flowers not bombs kind of thing? asked Jack. I don't know yet, said Julienne. Well, figure it out, he said. Or you'll bomb, flower.

C

On a sticky day at the end of July, Julienne came home with Chinese food from the place a block away, that despite the blurry bulletproof glazing indoors became one of their favorites: mapo tofu, which always reminded her of a video on rubber sap harvesting she had watched as a child, shrimp with black beans, scallion pancakes, gai lan in oyster sauce. She peered into the first room in their long hall; Gaspar had left the makeshift studio—all his now; it was too small and dark for them both to use—a wreck; wires everywhere, days of loathing shed, abandoned dishes, shredded paper as if she had moved in with a kindergarten's guinea pig. Bunny? she called from down the long hall. He was unlikely to hear her over the television, which was blasting awful news that she could not make out. When she reached the sitting room, Gaspar was wrapped in a blanket and had so compressed his height that his knees seemed to be at his nose. She set the bags of food on the table—which did not smell the way she had dreamed of an hour earlier—and sat on the floor to meet his face. Hey, she whispered. Are you all right? He said no. She asked, What's wrong? Hama, one of the largest cities in Syria, had been attacked late at night. It's Ramadan, you know? he said. Such cowards. It's the most beautiful place, with massive water wheels, probably what you think the Netherlands look like. Sorry, he said, catching himself. I'm so angry. Everyone living there is going to die. You don't know that, said Julienne. My host family are from there originally; I'm not sure that I told you. They came to Aleppo in the early eighties after the massacre, although that doesn't begin to describe it, he said. It was razed flat thirty years ago. I can hardly believe it still exists. If it does. Anyway, we went there once. Karim's brother was a musician, too. They would play late into the night in their garden. I've spent the rest of my life trying to recapture the peace of that moment, that place. They were so kind. I visited them again the last time I was in Syria. And that will be the last. I'll never find their graves to place flowers, and I have a hunch, he said, that maybe most of these places, lots of these people, children, you know, won't see the next decade. You start with warning shots, a few dissidents killed as deterrent, rubber bullets and tear gas, collateral, tanks, right, and then, then. He was shivering despite the heat. Gaspar, said Julienne, taking both his hands. You're freezing cold. That's okay, he said. I regret everything anyway. He excused himself to call his parents and shut himself into the cage.

D

On Friday she had plans to see a divorce movie that appeared to be about Rachel Weisz in the 1940s doing an excellent Anna Karenina. On the way out, she was called by human resources to a conference room on the tenth floor. It was unlikely to be a surprise party thrown by the Swiss assistant manager who introduced herself as Maud. Jürgen had been out of the office all week. On the phone he had been somewhat short with her but accepted her travel arrangements and was anyway often like that; no coldness or antipathy but an ordinary efficiency of speech and manner. Maud said, Your line manager has documented concerns about your behavior in the previous months and has decided that it will be best to close your relationship with the company. We have appreciated your contribution to the team and wish you the best in your future endeavors. Do you have any questions for me? Well, yes, said Julienne. Have any reasons been given? What have I done? While the complaints of your manager must remain confidential, Maud said, it seems that you have been late sixteen times in the previous four months. By a matter of minutes, but this position requires you to be logged into the computer system no later than 7:25 a.m., as you well know. There have also been complaints from the other administrative assistants about your relative unfriendliness and lack of engagement. She folded her hands in prayer over a folder with Julienne's name and ID number on it. Was that it? Maud's primary function was to protect Jürgen, what Julienne had been told was her own job. All right, Julienne said. Thank you. Maud said, Your health insurance will go through the end of next month. COBRA information will be sent to your home. You have provided the bank with seven years of service and as such will receive seven weeks' severance. Your next paycheck will include unused vacation days. Julienne asked, Shall I get my things? Maud said, Security will prepare and deliver them to you outside the front entrance.

NITROGEN SCALE

F ♯

Bob had asked what was bothering her. Julienne had smiled and said that work was tiring; it was tiring to clean houses, to clean offices, and to answer phones, which she always cleaned at the end of the day; it was tiring to live on the subway. She wasn't sure whether to tell him at all: Was it any of his business? She had asked Dr. Sarkarov. No, she had responded; this was her decision alone. Julienne had waited for the line on her watch to click to eleven. She was officially one week late. Her biological clock had a high-pitched voice, like a child's. She caught her reflection in a window: there was an undeniable contentedness in her face and a spring in her step; Julienne, finally, had joined humanity. At the drugstore she purchased three packs each from the company with the plus sign and the one with the lines; all six said yes. So as not to tip off her roommates, Julienne rinsed off the tests in the sink and put them in a bag to be disposed of in a public receptacle. She washed her hands several times and went to her bedroom to lie down, with her hands crossed over her chest as if she were watching clouds or dead. What if she did nothing for the next seven months, letting her belly swell, playing Mozart for the baby in utero. then raising them between the apartment she shared with two very young women and her mother's pink cowgirl house of neglect? For the next few days she imagined the becoming of a human being in her body, whose consciousness would be harnessed to flesh, her flesh, her blood, her cells; soft bones, soft head, stroking fine hair as the child wailed herself red as a currant, the excruciating knowledge of having brought death and suffering into the world. Julienne told Dr. Sarkarov that she couldn't ask a child to live on the subway as she did now, to wait as she groveled for

WIC and food stamps and Medicaid and housing vouchers once they were born. There was no shame in all that, said Dr. Sarkarov, but who said that she had to do any of it? On the way home, Julienne had a fantasy of raising a baby in a tiny house in Lübeck, growing vegetables, playing in the forest; she could keep a studio, build one herself, drive home materials and machinery. She could give the child all she never had—peaceful evenings, warm baths, bedtime stories, richly pigmented crayons—and the sensorial pleasures of new life, the piercing howl of new lungs: I am here. So when she called Planned Parenthood to schedule the abortion—the right thing to do, her only viable option at age thirty-four—the dream died. She would be extracting a cluster of cells from the body like any other. When asked whether she preferred a surgical or medical abortion, Julienne chose the former without hesitation— she would not bleed out a fetus for days on a toilet—and was booked in for the following Wednesday, six and a half weeks in, enough to hear a heartbeat. When the day came, she went to the center on Court Street; the line was long and there were layers of bulletproof glass to traverse; the waiting room was filled with women and a few crying infants. She had never been sure of what was in the Top 40 but now she knew. When her name was finally called, she put the fee on a credit card and was advised that the wait would be long. It was spent reading Susan Sontag's journal entries from 1967 (when the author had been thirty-four years old): as a child Sontag had thought that once she birthed her son, she would become a real mother but also a real adult; she would give birth to herself, but did this not mean therefore that the child would give birth to her? There was a shout from the corridor that might have been attributed to anything, but Julienne decided firmly to take the sedation. Who could take her home? Jennifer was, after all, a doctor but had patients till nine that evening; her youthful roommates would have distracting, spunky, politically charged responses; maybe one of the girls from the bank now that Julienne no longer worked there. Neither did Maggie, she thought, who had resigned from Oberschleißheim Bank AG to tend bar and audition for plays. Something wrong? Maggie said when she picked up. Julienne said, I have a favor to ask— I'm getting an abortion and they won't let me leave on my own after sedation. Could you help me out? I'll pay you, of course, she added, not sure how she could. Maggie said, Don't be ridiculous. I'm coming. Julienne said, There's a lot of security. Maggie laughed. Yeah, I know. Julienne went with Maggie's name to pay for the sedation; no, she hadn't eaten anything in days, thanks for asking.

G

She had just been offered a new job as the executive assistant to the CEO of an arts community center—it seemed stupid to her that such an organization should have a CEO, but maybe this was why she had no money—in Downtown Brooklyn and had to bite her lip from squealing in delight. It was only the first week, but she had a nice-enough boss who had facilitated her enrollment in a heavily discounted blacksmithing class; she had always envied the students chiseling away at hot orange metal, holding massive instruments high over their heads in front of some kind of oven. What power! What deltoids! At Dr. Sarkarov's office she began the session fantasizing about the things she would make; she could not wait for her first horseshoe. You know that Freud was born over a blacksmithing shop. He used to wonder what became of all the unsuccessful tinkers, and gunsmiths, and shoemakers, and blacksmiths; but nobody could ever tell him, said Dr. Sarkarov. Freud wondered about that? Julienne asked. No, said Dr. Sarkarov. Mark Twain, as cited by Freud, writing about Adler. OK, said Julienne. What do you make of wanting to take this class? Dr. Sarkarov asked. Do you intend to work with metal or shoe horses or what? I often used to work with sheet metal in graduate school, Julienne said. I enjoyed all the soldering and welding, fusing things together. Something strikes me about your interests, Dr. Sarkarov said. You don't like natural materials. Julienne asked, Really? What's so unnatural about metal and glass? Ores. Sand. We all ingest metals, to live. Salts. Metal is also fragile. It rusts. It bends. Dr. Sarkarov said, You also work in plastics and resins. Julienne said, Sure. Dr. Sarkarov said, It's striking that you prefer to work with industrial materials. I was interested in the unnatural processes they demanded, said Julienne. They were outside the ordinary human activities. They planned our obsolescence.

A ◁

Willa had a friend named Suzanne; they were both single and of the same age and would go out dancing while Julienne stayed with Suzanne's blue-haired grandmother, who smoked and sat her with Oreos on a matted pink carpet in front of the mid-eighties *Twilight Zone* revival. Julienne cared for neither of those things: Rosie—as Julienne called her—was there, the love of her life. She was a stray dog who wandered the neighborhood; a mix of everything: wolf, poodle, husky, Great Dane, fox, according to Suzanne, although Julienne knew already that this could not be true—her big eyes and long, soft black curls seemed to have emerged, in this ugly place, from a kind of magic; Rosie had no ancestry and belonged to no one except for (she hoped) Julienne; she had roamed the roads and chose this house when she was there, with its compressed backyard, littered lightly with household garbage. Julienne would go out to greet Princess Rosie with smuggled tennis balls and hot dogs from supper in hand. When Willa came for Julienne in the early hours of the morning, she would often find her curled up on the floor next to Rosie and wake them with her unsober laughter. Often Rosie growled back. One twilit morning, as Julienne and her mother were getting into the car, Rosie darted past the door to rescue Julienne and was stricken immediately by a Buick, which braked hard. Julienne screamed and threw herself in front of the car over Rosie's body as she bled everything into her arms. The driver came out, apologizing profusely. Julienne's mother said, It's okay, sweetie. There will be so many just like her.

B ♩

For the first six months, they stayed at Gaspar's parents' apartment, which was normally rented out for a few months at a time through an agency. Eventually there emerged a studio on East Ninth Street between Tompkins Square Park and Avenue C that fell within their price range; someone in Gaspar's cohort needed someone to take over his lease after he bought a place. It was the kind of never-updated abode that fit the trappings of rent stabilization: peeling latex paint that covered old lead paint, rusty window grates, loose and water-damaged floorboards, holes and leaks and cracks, waivers for asbestos and lead, mold, mold, mold. Gaspar had suggested that his dad would be willing to do an inspection with an engineer friend and help with some repairs. They could fund the rest themselves, do a little DIY and make it a tolerable home. What about all your allergies? Julienne asked. This place could kill you. Oh, said Gaspar. I mean, I guess I could wear protective gear. We can wear hazmat suits everywhere. All the time. Like all. The. Time. You're so—She cut herself off and laughed. He said, we also don't yet have to move—but I know the situation makes you uncomfortable. I feel gross mooching off of your parents, she said. Your mother also hates me. Gaspar said, My mother finds you very precise— high praise—and my dad likes anyone who has fun with heavy industrial materials. I wish that you didn't care so much about what they think, Julienne said. No, I'm saying that you seem to worry about it, but who cares, really, said Gaspar, before singing in the worst, scratchiest Springsteen impression she'd ever heard, I'd take a stray bullet for you . . . a domesticated one, too! She laughed.

That's not a song. That's how you love a Jersey girl, said Gaspar. Isn't it?

C

Leïla invited Julienne over for lunch in early September, just after Gaspar's departure to Los Angeles. The cook was off, she apologized, but they had plenty of Waldorf salad left over from dinner the night before. The dining room—facing north, with large windows—had long been repurposed as an art studio, which would be unremarkable but for Leïla's love of dinner parties, which took place in a long, wide hall on the other side of the dwelling as if it were a banqueting house. There were rooms with tables that Julienne had never seen in the years of their friendship—also unremarkable but for Leïla's love of house tours—but they ate on the finely tiled terrace outside, which looked into a manicured garden. The apartment belonged to Leïla's parents, and given that Julienne's analogous experience with Gaspar's parents' home on the Upper West Side had been brief, modest, and in the distant past, she felt terribly for Axel. Is the wine okay? Leïla asked. It's leftover Chablis. Thanks, said Julienne (who would have chosen gewürztraminer), it's great. Leïla asked, How are you doing with the move? I'm all right, said Julienne. We're not sure whether to set up there for good. He's coming back at Thanksgiving; he was granted an early sabbatical this spring to finish a book and some other work: a film score, something at the Oslo Opera House. But he'll be here, mostly. Leïla said, Wow, he never told me about Oslo. One of his many, many, many festivals, said Julienne, smiling. You will never meet a man more festive than Gaspar. They both laughed. Ugh, I can't imagine being a musician, said Leïla. Imagine having to collaborate with so many people. How's the new job? Julienne asked. Good, said Leïla. I love the department. My commute is terrible, but I would rather die than live in New Haven. Besides, she added, I get to see a lot of Ali and Sana—they really miss Gaspar and I guess I'm the closest thing. That's nice, said Julienne, who had not heard from them in months. I thought Gaspar would be allergic to Los Angeles, said Leïla, but maybe it'll loosen him up a little. She leaned back and looked at Julienne. I just can't see you there, either. Julienne asked, Would you live in LA? Leïla said, Oh, of course—there I would rule the world; so few proper curators out west. When they finished eating, Leïla brought her to the territorialized dining room studio; she had been working for many years on reworkings of the history of Orientalist art and had finally arrived at the massive French paintings in the Salle Mollien at the Louvre. Her face on Marianne's in *Liberty Leading the People*, her face on all the men in *The Raft of the Medusa*—she would be cannibalizing herself—her face on all the men and women in *The Death of Sardanapalus*, violating and murdering herself. Leïla showed Julienne the start of *Women of Algiers in Their Apartment*. Certainly I am the three women from the harem, she explained. But I am also the African servant pulling back the drapes. Julienne was offended but suspected that this was part of Leïla's provocation. That's nice, said Julienne. Leïla said, Wait, you have an MFA, don't you? Yes, said Julienne, but it's been a while. Have you made anything since then? Leïla asked. Not really, said Julienne. Oh my god! Leïla squealed. I just remembered that you used to model in college. Would you sit for me? Julienne laughed. Not unless you have any desks built like tanks for me to pose with, she said. Better still if you have a rotary telephone. Of course we do, said Leïla. They're antiques. Ugh, I hate when wine sweetens, she continued, plonking down her glass on a taboret. This tastes like gewürztraminer.

D ◁

Gaspar said, All right, so I've come to settle the bills—We have time for that, interjected Julienne. Excuse me, said Gaspar. Our lease ends in April. I've paid my half through the end directly to the landlord so you won't have to worry about my deposit. He'll separately send it to our accounts. Fine, said Julienne. She ladled the liver dumplings into soup bowls and brought them to the table. As she returned for the cucumber salad, Gaspar inquired, Is it all right if I don't eat all of this? Sure, said Julienne. The buzzer rang. God, she said. I hope that's not Andreas. Gaspar said, It is, probably. I can stall him for a bit. He took out his phone and began to type. Anyway, we can handle the termination of domestic partnership form later; if you need me to sign something to get off your health insurance, let me know. I don't want to end on a sour note. I'm sorry, said Julienne. I resented you for being so far away. Then Christmas—did we really need to invite Axel and Leïla? That may be so, said Gaspar. It may also be the reason why I don't know you anymore. You know me better than anyone in the world, said Julienne. Gaspar sighed. Well, I'm sorry to disappoint you, but that's a bit depressing, he said. Julienne's jaw dropped. Is this still about Syria? Gaspar said, You carefully chose your fighting instrument, if you will, and made it seem like an outburst. You chose the thing of no personal relevance to yourself, that, in addition to the death and displacement of millions, has destroyed the lives of—and probably killed; I try and try and hear nothing from anyone—people I love in a place of profound personal meaning . . . we have to end this now, I realized, because you will never understand that pain: it is as irreconcilable to me as a stab wound. Maybe worse. You know that wasn't what I meant to do, said Julienne. Honestly, Jules, said Gaspar, despite the stomach virus and your disappearance on Boxing Day—I told you I was leaving, said Julienne. Your parents' house at Christmas-time isn't a place for us to talk. Excuse me, said Gaspar. You clearly wanted to leave as soon as you got there. I'm glad you did because this—here he waved his arms about the room—doesn't make sense anymore. Some of that is the distance, especially now that I'm in LA, but you've made no effort to look for a job out there. I can't relo-cate, but you can. And in any case, many of my colleagues manage long distances and frankly it's just—I keep thinking that we're like two broken bones fused together in the wrong way. Do you know what I'm saying? That isn't true, said Julienne. Listen, said Gaspar. It's been eleven years. We grew up together. There were times when you literally kept me alive—often I think you regret it. It's unfortunate that things ended the way that they did, but it's simply illogical for us to continue in this manner. The buzzer rang again. All right, said Gaspar. That's Andreas. He's parked awkwardly. Come on, said Julienne. Gaspar raised his voice for the first time. I came to say what I wanted to and cannot continue repeating myself all night. I have to work tomorrow. Don't you, on the—here he waved again—executive floor?

He stood up, pushed in his chair, and went down the hall to open the door. Julienne left behind their revolting meal and went into the bedroom. Not a thing of his in it remained: How? When? Through the door she heard grunting and scraping and shuffling and thuds with lots of cursing. She wept into the soft surfaces so not to be heard. She wanted to suffocate. Eventually there was a hard knock at the door. Julienne swallowed hard. Yes? she called out. I'm leaving, Gaspar said. Julienne opened the door. He embraced her with more warmth than she expected and softly kissed her cheek. We'll be in touch, said Julienne. Stay well, said Gaspar.

E ♯

I saw you, more than one year after you died, at the Rubin Museum. They were showing *Hiroshima Mon Amour* under the pretense of an emoji theme. It was 😫 week and a young psychologist spoke about anger and maybe climate change. As you know, Willa claims that I was conceived as a direct result of watching this film, the one from the night I saw you after you died, on Betamax, with a surgeon from Hong Kong, in a hotel room in Kowloon. Every time I see it, I look for clues. Deductive reasoning indicates that my mother paid little attention to a film with subtitles, but my middle name, which I seldom use, is the same as the lead actress's: a tasteless combination, with a dizzying number of loops (how Leïla ridiculed me for it), which my mother thought would turn me beautiful. There was a raffle to win a book about environmental destruction that I didn't enter. Instead I wrote on the entry form: The city at ten thousand degrees / steel rendered flesh / nothing for me to weep over / I am not endowed with memory. When the film ended and the lights came on, there you were, at a table with a group of people. I turned around to watch without getting up. You squeezed the shoulders of a woman whose accent I couldn't make out, fifty feet from normal conversation. It didn't sound like one of your languages, but it was not inconceivable that if highly motivated you could learn Spanish or Italian or Portuguese in four years; after all, you had only been dead for one of them. You had the same gait and giggled like a child. Afterward I went to a diner and ordered calamari coated in blue corn flour with a cheap, syrupy glass of pinot grigio and saw you again, this time shorter, with lighter hair, bearded and bespectacled, very young, in pink jeans. You might have thought me an old woman if I talked to you; a nosy tourist. You ordered a beer, in English, with a different Spanish or Italian or Portuguese accent. If you are everywhere, this means that I am at once forgetting you and never will.

F ♯

Maggie entered the room with knitting needles poking out from a *Granta* tote bag; she seemed so far away in this vast, full space. In human terms, Julienne had felt that pregnancy was endless: division and division till a sentience was reached; this was what she was about to do, to abort the possibility of sentience; it was a natural, disappointing process shared by so many things: showers of blossom on the sidewalk, the squashed fruits of summer, red-dot-fresh eggs. In this process Julienne would return life to its liquid state: better this than the violence of childbirth, the pain of being alive, of illness, of cruelty, of real death. She stood up when Maggie reached her. No, no, sit, said Maggie. You'll be tired from all the drugs. Well, thanks for coming, said Julienne. Maggie shrugged. The chair across from Julienne became vacant. Maggie sat there, not knitting but reading a Richard Brautigan novel. When her name was finally called, she and Maggie went down a long corridor. The examination room made her stomach drop; it was like every OB-GYN office she had seen but enormous and encircled by machines. The nurse asked Maggie if she was Julienne's partner, and when she said no, the nurse said that she could wait outside if she wanted. Go ahead, Julienne said. Are you sure? Maggie asked. Yes, of course, said Julienne. I'll see you soon. The nurse asked Julienne if she had yet seen a doctor. When Julienne said no, the nurse nodded as if this were typical. Twenty-nine minutes after she left, a phlebotomist came in to draw blood. When the first pinprick went into her left elbow, Julienne began to blink back tears. It's okay, sweetheart, said the phlebotomist. You're going to be OK. She filled a plastic cup with water and gave it to Julienne before squeezing her shoulder on the way out. Once alone, Julienne began to rave like a ghost: Would she, who had donated twenty of her own eggs as a student, whose fertility status was unknown, who might never have this chance again, who was not well-off but healthy enough at least to raise a child, do this decisively final thing; would she ever have been in this situation had she not murdered off Gaspar like a Gorgon, he who had not managed to stay alive for his own child? How she loathed Bob! After forty-six minutes, she heard a knock at the door. Clear-throated, Julienne said, come in. I'm Dr. Berg, said the white-coated, curly-headed woman who entered the room. She shook Julienne's hand and confirmed what she was going to do. First I'll do an ultrasound—would you like to look? No, said Julienne, declining to do what she felt would be the brave thing to do, to look herself in the eye. Thanks, she added. She turned away her neck. Dr. Berg said, simply, Mmm-hmm. Mmm-hmm. Mmm-hmm. All right, said Dr. Berg. The nurse anesthetist will be in shortly; the procedure will take no fewer than fifteen minutes. You, having opted for sedation, will spend one hour in the recovery room. Julienne thanked her again. Alone she began to talk silently to the being in her belly.

She said that she was sorry, that they deserved better than she could give, that she knew their soul, more beautiful than she knew how to manage, would return to the world. The creature spoke back. It said that it understood, that it had loved living in her belly, but now it was time to go. She thanked them. Dr. Berg returned with the nurse who took in Julienne and the anesthetist who would put her out. She remembered nothing after that in the recovery room, behind a drape, lighthearted and numb. There was a tray behind the recliner in which she was sat with water and a small cup of pills—ibuprofen and something for nausea—and maxi pads with branded literature. A nurse approached to ask Julienne how she was and tell her to monitor her bleeding, to avoid large meals. She offered a sugary drink, dry crackers, a heating pad. Julienne got dressed and went to meet Maggie in the waiting area. How are you feeling? she asked. I don't know what that means, thought Julienne, who said, Just fine, thanks. Here, said Maggie, handing Julienne a sheaf of papers. These are care instructions for the next few days, like don't fuck the guy who did this to you. Outside Maggie hailed them a taxi and gave the driver the address Julienne had written out for her. Maggie helped Julienne to unlock the front door and up the stairs into the apartment. Both the roommates were home. Oh my god, said Emma. You look so tired! Are you okay? Yes, said Julienne. Just tired. Did you have your wisdom teeth taken out? Ashley asked. Something like that, said Maggie. Julienne gestured toward her bedroom. Maggie opened it and flopped into the armchair at the window. Wow, dude, she said. You have the cleanest bedroom. How do you sleep in here? God, said Julienne. I feel so heavy. Lie down, said Maggie. Do you need help? No, no, thank you for everything, said Julienne. Yeah, it's okay, said Maggie. Julienne fell asleep. When she woke it was four thirty in the morning and pitch-dark; for the previous twelve hours she had been crumpled into an irregular dodecahedron and everything hurt. In the bathroom she saw that she had saturated the pad and the sides of her jeans. She showered, washed her face, brushed her teeth, then looked in the mirror for relief or regret and saw neither.

ARSENIC SCALE

E ◁

You began to take Arsenicum Album 30c just after your first semester in Los Angeles. I went to meet you at LaGuardia and in the taxi you knocked back five little dots, a hybridization of several childhood candies. Perhaps you had different ones. Reflexively, I had nearly smacked the small blue canister away from your hand; you took so many pills every day. You told me that they were no different from the arnica cream I had used on the lightbulb bruises that you gave me slash that I gave myself, or the zinc tablets under the tongue to ward off colds. Should a Teutonophile like yourself not love homeopathy? you asked. But what is it for? I had asked. You said, Stomach troubles, all right? I got drunk and ate some nightshades. What do you mean? I asked. Mushrooms? No, you said, exasperated. You had eaten salsa, potato chips, and baba ghanoush at a John Lautner house owned by a Hollywood music producer of whom I had not heard, but should have, apparently. Such a gathering had nightshades? I asked incredulously. Then you got angry. If you ate as little as I did, you said, you wouldn't have any problems, but since you had a normal person's appetite . . . I tried to calm you down, but your face was so hot, I thought you might really be sick. Okay, I said. We have ginger root at home, I'll make you tea. You said, I don't know, what if I become inured to ginger? Then you caught yourself and said, In Soviet Russia, ginger becomes inured to you, took my hand, and kissed me for real. I was sad, angry, and tired, but did my duty and smiled, for you.

F

She did not know what to do with the information. Reporting a death in the family, Julienne called out to the office-cleaning agency, the home-cleaning agency, and the office-temp agency. In her chest and belly were something like awe; this was what horror was: something in her rejected this information; he was gone. He had left behind husks and hollows, gleaming superficially with health, to the coroner but in the way that he had willed could not be found anywhere in the world. What had happened; had a quack doctor in Los Angeles finally bungled his mix of antihistamines, antidepressants, anticonvulsants, antipsychotics, anxiolytics, corticosteroids, mast cell stabilizers, mood stabilizers, tranquilizers, and all those stupid, tiny hippie drugs; had a Norwegian doctor, converting them to approved legal alternatives, made a mistake; had he become trapped in his own mind, forcing everyone around him to speak their second language perfectly just for him; were the extreme emotions of parenthood and its accompanying responsibility at once too much to bear and too much to abandon, leaving the zero sum to suicide—here she shook her head; that had hardly been confirmed—for that matter, who had let him do any of that; didn't anyone know him; who had let him marry, have a child, and move to a beautiful and peaceful country that was also frigid, pitch-dark, and filled with petroleum? She drew the shades and blinds and spent the rest of the day under the duvet trying to block out all the light, not sleeping, nearly calling Ali and Sana to offer condolences but hanging up just before the call was connected, nearly desperate enough to call Leïla. Then, when she ceased these nervous activities, she cried to the point of vomiting; after scarcely having made it to the bathroom, Julienne showered and washed her face and brushed her teeth. Where to go? What had he liked? Where could she find him? The Spanish medieval gardens at the Cloisters where he had taken her the first day of winter break in college, their first real home on Ninth Street, the small spaces they never seemed to visit twice where his favorite musicians would play late into the night, the shop in SoHo with all the old guitars, the performance spaces in Brooklyn at which she had often stood to the side, waiting for something to happen. Then she changed her mind: she should connect with death. What made her want to die? Julienne called her mother. Can I come over? she asked. It's Wednesday, said Willa. What's wrong? Did you get fired? No, Julienne said. Well, I can't get you from the train station tonight. Come tomorrow, Willa said. Okay, Julienne said. What happened? Willa asked. Julienne's voice cracked. She swallowed hard a sob. Gaspar's dead, Julienne said. She began again to cry. Oh, Julie, Willa said. Just imagine; you could have been a widow.

G

After they had touched the voting screens everywhere a Democrat should, Bob had asked her about all the coughing. It was not abnormal to have a tickle in one's throat in November, Julienne said. Allergies, probably. He asked if they should go out to watch the election results in a bar that night, but she said that she was going to the studio for a few hours after work and would see him at home. The truth was that Julienne had taken the day off to undergo a thoracoscopy. She would need a few hours to recover, said the hospital staff member scheduling the event. Was there anyone who could help her home? No, Julienne had said. A spiraling CT scan had showed a soft shadow, poking out like a spring crocus from beneath the breastbone like a flower between two Gaudí vaults. Her eyes had wandered over the bloom from all the angles the camera had captured. She had coughed honestly into a cup. The pulmonologist had told her that she would perform a biopsy of the mass as well as some of the surrounding tissue and one of her lymph nodes. She would sample and drain the fluid if there were any. She would make three incisions: one under the shoulder blade, one under her arm, and one beneath the breast. She was afraid: a woman with whom she had gone to college (a dancer turned yoga teacher) had died during a routine endoscopy, but Julienne had so little to lose were she to die on the table. The anesthesiologist had a beautiful smile and asked Julienne what her favorite color was. Julienne said silver, mumbling late winter and green shoots. Out of caution she had stayed in the recovery room until six. It was a mockingly beautiful dark blue November night. Functionally groggy from the anesthetic, with three new canalizations into her left lung with tubal extensions into the world, placated with oxycodone and enormous ibu-profens, she did not hurt for the first time in years. Despite herself, she smiled. There seemed to be a giddy energy in the air. Women and girls were out, free, unself-conscious. In perhaps five hours, the most qualified person ever to have run, who had faced nearly continuous public assault her entire adult life, would become the first woman president. Julienne's mother had always loathed her. Gaspar had always loathed her. Bob had held his nose and touched the screen. Julienne, suddenly, was euphoric. She stopped in her favorite Japanese café for a twiggy tea and onigiri and afterward nearly skipped to the F. On the other side she got out two stops early, for the notorious sign she had been reading about, at the intersection of President and Clinton Streets. It would be a funny souvenir of the day, of the era. She struggled with the front-facing camera: it was impossible, in such a small window, to capture her face and the sign far above her head. A woman with a stroller offered to help; as she squinted at the shutter two middle-aged men passed and looked Julienne up and down. She's not worth it, one said to the other. Julienne thanked the woman and offered to take a photograph of her. She declined. As Julienne walked up Clinton Street, her rib cage began to ache, a sign of some other pain, so she stopped in the park to take more ibuprofen. It was still lively. Somehow she found a bench. There were families with dogs and children and young people with signs. She realized suddenly that Bob would ask about the tubes and bandages and opioids and that she had packaged them, inadvertently, as a twisted surprise. Everyone who surrounded her in the park gleamed with health. In the distance she heard cheers each time a state was called. Julienne decided that if she did indeed have cancer, however treatable, she would not burden—or even tell—anyone. She had left no imprint on the world and could will herself to evaporate. When she came home at around ten, Julienne asked Bob about the election results. It's weirdly close, he said. He muted the television. Are you okay? Yes, Julienne said. Just tired. She went into the bathroom to wash her face, brush her teeth, and tend to her wounds, concealing the detritus in billowing paper. When she came out, Bob announced that he was worried about Michigan and encouraged her to sit down. Don't worry, Julienne said. She went into the bedroom and shut the door behind her.

A

There was some kind of property dispute between the two big farmers in their town at the border between New Jersey and Pennsylvania, the Torellis and the McArdles, and on day three one of the Torellis' milking cows were found dead, shot cleanly in the heart. Katie Torelli never again showed up to school. One week later, all the hens at the McArdle Farm—the field trip destination every other year—had been poisoned. Willa had told her not to worry; it wasn't as if Julienne were a hen or a milking cow. What about Katie? Julienne asked. Maybe they thought she would squeal to the cops, Willa joked. This did very little to assuage Julienne's fears. One afternoon in art class they watched a film strip about Richard Serra. (The art teacher was adjunct faculty at the fancy college across the Pennsylvania border and taught all the students in the middle school every Friday.) The jocks in the back spent the time shooting spitballs into the ugly girls' hair. Julienne was about to rat them out, but her thoughts were interrupted by what she saw on the screen. Serra had made a list of infinitives, not that Julienne knew back then what an infinitive was, and a few prepositions (of which they had learned). These would become actions on material: to splash, to swirl, to bounce, of nature. He poured molten lead all over the floor. His assistant dropped lead from up high for him to catch. His steel sculptures weighed tons and tons and had killed one installer and severely injured two others. His works were enormous, impossible to ignore, and often vandalized. They inspired awe and also hurt. Afterward, the teacher gave them thin sheets of Bristol board and instructed them to act on Serra's verb list in ten different ways. The boys in the back burst out laughing because they had spent the whole session rolling, crumpling, splashing, and spilling and were done. Julienne was choosing from the list when an announcement came from the PA system. They were all asked to meet in the auditorium. The principal, school nurse, and guidance counselor were onstage. The principal announced that Katie Torelli had been found injured but alive, a thousand miles away in Missouri. The town, nevertheless, had indefinitely imposed a curfew from dusk till dawn. Any evening school activities would be canceled—plays, concerts, dances—and any classes involving the wood or metal shop.

B ♩

They had moved together to New York in August 2001, the site of Gaspar's first-choice doctoral program in composition. Six weeks later, Gaspar had nearly arrived at the music school on East Third Street at which he taught guitar lessons when he got out of the subway station to gulp the outdoor air that would burn his chest. He was not sure what he was looking at but for the scale of swarming, thick black clouds streaking the sky and no one being able to outwalk or outrun the crowd, which ran only north. For a moment he thought that the particles that made up the black clouds were human, and then that this was not so far from the truth. Was this a dream, or was he dead? He assumed that a series of bombs had gone off till he struck up a conversation with the man shuffling next to him, Elias, a cab driver from Lebanon who explained to him that one plane had crashed into the Twin Towers, then another. Elias offered him a ride but it seemed evident that they would not get very far. The odor seared the memory of any others Gaspar had known. He tried to call Julienne (temping in a midtown office building), then his parents, but his cell phone was dead. Any one of them, he thought, please. At Grand Central he and his new friend were about to part ways when a woman kicked Gaspar, hard, in the bare left calf, from behind. Paki idiot, she spat in punctuation, walking away hand in hand with her husband. Why is everyone after Pakistan? asked Elias. Why not North Korea? Later Gaspar diagonally crossed Central Park. Two hours later he was outside the small apartment his parents were lending him and Julienne, who was sat on the stoop and about to embrace him when she inhaled hard and asked what was on his leg: he hadn't noticed the sharp, still-wet wound. She held him for a bit too long. Upstairs they had left the curtains drawn in the morning rush. Normally Julienne liked to throw open all the windows but the air was so different now. She told Gaspar to let her clean the cut but he shook his head and lay gash-side down so that she couldn't see it. He was damp everywhere and smelled slightly of raw mushrooms.

C

They were given permission by the management to replace the broken ceiling fan in the living room with a pendant lamp if they paid the materials and labor themselves. Together they had selected a simple composition of clear globes, fashionable in its day. Their stepladder was not tall enough; Julienne couldn't see everything she needed to so they kept trading places. She was no electrician, but Gaspar was all opposable thumb, and when he finally got the exposed bulb to light again, he was fleetingly blinded and dropped one of the globes from the ceiling fan onto Julienne's nose. She shrieked. The object bounced and fell to the floor without shattering. Its spritely movement lent the incident an ugly slapstick and she was in such shock that they laughed. He asked if she was all right, and she said yes; the throbbing pain was not so different from stubbing one's toe. She pressed some ice over her nose but it was time to leave: Gaspar was playing gamelan in a new trio with violin and cello that evening. They were silent on the subway to Brooklyn: Gaspar preferred to listen to previous recordings before the performance, which mystified Julienne as they seemed to stress him out; she distracted herself from the aching of her nose by counting different things—exposed toenails, corrosion around screws, letters X in advertisements. They had enough time to stand in front of a Mexican-French gastropub whilst Gaspar scanned the menu for the relative dearth of potatoes, tomatoes, eggplants, and other nightshades. Julienne began to gaze blankly across the road at a shop that sold tiled carpeting and a baby store that sold hand-carved rocking horses from Iceland, where Gaspar had gone earlier that summer. There was tension around her eyes, and her nose no longer felt as if it belonged to her body. You have a stockpile of those under our bed, don't you? asked Gaspar. Of what? Julienne asked. Baby clothes, said Gaspar. For whom? asked Julienne. For you? Gaspar said, There's nothing on this menu that I can eat. Julienne said, You were the one who suggested the all-tomato restaurant. And you didn't think to stop me? Gaspar sighed. I need to set up. Why don't you have something and wait here? I'll find an energy bar or something. Julienne said, I think I should go to the emergency room—my nose is really sore. There's a lot of pressure. He said, Okay. Okay. I'll come find you afterward. Shouldn't you come with me? She demanded. But I have a concert, he said. Isn't this an emergency? she asked. You'll be fine, said Gaspar. You dropped a glass bulb on my nose, said Julienne. Obviously, you were supposed to catch it, he said. She repeated, You dropped a heavy piece of glass on my nose! He said, Why didn't you say anything earlier? Julienne said, Don't you have a hundred gongs to set up? He sighed and went to the convenience store to look for an energy bar. Julienne went to the nearest hospital and then straight home with a bandage on her nose. In the weeks that followed, they would laugh about it together with Gaspar's friends and acquaintances, like they were in *The Three Stooges*, but at work Julienne would say she fell.

D

Julienne was relieved that Willa had gone to Florida for Thanksgiving: this meant that she could now see the new divorce movie advertised during a viewing of *Boyhood*. The Saturday night after it opened, she wore a snowflake sweater under her trench to greet the premature autumnal nip and smuggled into the Paris Theater harissa olives and a Knusperflakes Ritter Sport for the first of the three versions: They, then Her, then Him; five hours of divorce—she could not wait. The heroine with the beautiful bones had fallen into a horrible depression following the death of their son, plunged from the Manhattan Bridge, and survived. She had preferred to return to her childhood home in Connecticut (perhaps an hour away from Gaspar's) rather than the Astor Place apartment she shared with her callow husband. She sliced her hair into a copper crop and began to commute to Cooper Union (which seemed unlikely to be for her, as a lapsed doctoral candidate in anthropology), which meant that she often unwillingly ran into her ex. It was also not far from the first apartment Julienne and Gaspar truly shared, with all the same references: Gaspar's old music school, Gaspar's old studio, Cooper Square, Saint Mark's Bookshop (which, of course, had moved), the flashy new building at Cooper Union that seemed nice until she found out why it existed and then it became very ugly, the disconnected uptown 6. And now Gaspar was in Oslo, not the café in Brooklyn, in Norway, married to an opera singer who was the daughter of a famous architectural theorist. Julienne squirmed in her seat at the proximity of the fictional couple's intimate memories to hers and then felt so hollow: there was nothing original to their own story, her own life; she did not know how one felt sufficiently loved, nor how to return another person's love. Eleven years with Gaspar and she had stormed off perhaps three hundred times and he had followed her nearly as many into the cold dark; he had stood up for her in front of his family, friends, and odious colleagues as well as Julienne's mother. She considered the stories of kings and queens who ingested small amounts of poison to prevent being killed and snake charmers with venom tattoos. When she returned to the theater three weeks later to watch Her, then Him, she was surprised to be bored and regretted not having brought more snacks.

E ◁

You still chastised me for the smile and called it saving face, which was surprising, given your newfound sunshine. But the sun leaches water from grass, sears the unpigmented splotch on your neck, massacres the flowers and the wolves, crumbles the soil, sacrifices the innocent to vultures. I read about prisoners of war forced to kneel or lie before the master—the bright sun at midday—and stare for more than thirty minutes at a time over consecutive days; if they refused they were electrocuted or sprayed with poisons. You preferred the moon, you said, and the stars; in mock horror I said that of course you did, you wanted to control the tides and oceans. You loved the light on the new snow, not when it gleamed and shocked but the softness with which it was absorbed into the gentle surface. It doesn't snow in New

York anymore, really; if the gods gave all the snow to you, wherever you are, I wouldn't mind. This was how you were found: sometimes I dream that you simply froze to death, that you curled up into the snow in the soft dark and surrendered.

CEMENT SCALE

F ♮

Halloween fell on the night before daylight saving time began. Julienne's roommates were throwing a party and had begged her to come, suggesting several three-person costumes—the Witches of Eastwick, the Real-Symbolic-Imaginary, Dvořák's Horn Trio—in which to participate, so Julienne faked a retirement party and donated them a bottle of vodka. There was nothing she wanted to see at the theaters closest to her but she discovered that *Pather Panchali* and *Aparajito* were playing back-to-back at Film Forum. She had seen the former once in her first year of college: the older drama student she was dating said that if she liked De Sica she would love Ray although she had said nothing about liking De Sica and he corrected himself by saying that as a member of the proletariat that she would not only love De Sica but really love Ray. She did remember the actors' faces; few were professionals and nearly everything had been improvised. On the short walk from the subway she ran into the annual Halloween parade and was trampled by a Superman. The doorman at the bar in front of which she fell offered his barstool but she forced herself to the theater. There she bought a large peppermint tea and a slice of lemon-poppy sponge cake that the card said had been praised by Derrida. The theater was not empty—filled with others skipping out on Halloween and retirement parties—but Julienne was able to find a row to herself in the front. She smiled to herself at the opening scenes when Durga reluctantly left the forest to help her mother and Julienne remembered Gaspar's own vexing charms, in that very room of that very theater ten years earlier at a crowded screening of *The Earrings of Madame D . . .* , at which he convinced an entire row of cinemagoers to move over so that they could sit together and everyone smiled. Everyone that evening was still smiling: the siblings played charming pranks on one another in the rain, and when, in effect, the rain killed Durga in her father's absence—perhaps the most important plot detail Julienne could have forgotten—she felt as if her heart was being squeezed in mesh and a full-body heave clamped and welded the material in all directions, which did not stop her from watching the second film, from which the audience had dissipated slightly but was perhaps even more beautiful than the first, against the striking ghats, until Apu's father died, shocking away a flock of birds, and, finally, the death of Apu's mother, slumped, nearly awake, against a tree, which brought a kind of nausea but no relief.

G

Julienne now lived in an empty (but for boxes, suitcases, and an air mattress) one-room apartment in Sunset Park, two blocks from the ceramics studio. One week after the election, Bob was due to take her for a birthday dinner.

Julienne had said that she was not in a celebratory mood. She told him over pizza only that she was unhappy, that their situation was no longer working, and that she wished him the very best. I found a place already, she said, and will be out before the end of the month. He had nodded and said that he would need to retain her security deposit. She asked why he had gone on vacation with Heike. He said that her grief over Gaspar's death was a boundary that he could not cross to her, that the situation was too close to his uncle's overdose, that Heike was family. Julienne had smiled politely and said, Well, why don't you occupy yourself with all that. You're cruel, Bob had said. I know, Julienne had said with a sigh. I'm sorry. She had paid the bill and slept on the sofa for most of the two weeks left; having rid herself of any remaining furniture before going to live with Bob there was little packing to do but for some clothes from Bob's chest of drawers. Everything else remained in boxes. While waiting for the movers, Julienne paged through a book that had caught her eye when she first started dating Bob and couldn't sleep, about a mathematician-novelist who could not write a book about the Great Fire of London however he interpolated or bifurcated the manuscript in part because he was still grieving the death of his young wife, which did not stop him from developing his own law of the perfect butter croissant but also because he was trying to avoid spectacular, catastrophic failure. Was she cruel? she asked herself, sketching in front of a space heater at the ceramics studio. How important was it to avoid spectacular, catastrophic failure in the face of one's own death; was it best not to try or to leave behind wretched, murderous disappointment; was the latter in itself cruel, an abuse of space, materials, and the human spirit? She reckoned that it didn't matter: the worst that would happen was that her work would be destroyed. Were she to drop dead in the ceramics studio, perhaps a bit of it would be left on display for a few months with a sticky note and the dates of her life if anyone there knew them. And so this became her life; with nothing but space she threw, glazed, and fired clay at the ceramics studio, used the force left in her lungs to blow glass and of her shoulders to hone metal and at home she glued and screwed together bits of construction (and set cement with organic aggregates) before returning to the ceramics studio to compose the larger assembly, which was beginning to blow out its corner of the room. Already seven feet by nine feet by eight feet of largely solid mass—there were perforations one might leverage to climb were the work not so fragile—it became a gleeful spectacle in that shop of delicacy. She needed all twenty-eight of the teeth that remained in her mouth, and her hair would be gone in time—she might destroy it in some resin, she thought, when the time came—but for now the work contained within everything she had.

A ♮

Julienne did not begin to study German until the first year of college. She had been persuaded by her advisor and classmates that studying art history would not keep her from law school, and the courses in the department catalog that most interested her concerned German, Swiss, and Viennese artists. In school she had done French but found it imprecise (baguette referred to too many things); German was elegant and efficient, like a blade: at least sections of verbs went at the start of each sentence, each noun began with a capital letter, there were three genders and four cases. One could not help but to say what one meant. She switched to the accelerated introductory class in the first week after seeing a poster advertising the college's JYA at a university in Berlin. Two years later she arrived: however the pictures materialized in her mind, whatever fantasies she had concocted from films or books or photographs, she could not have been prepared for the exhilaration of what surrounded her. The city was at once hundreds of years old and aged ten; the capital had moved that year from Bonn to Berlin. Cranes hung from the sky, demolition everywhere she went, and art: to her everything was so new that she had little concept of what was deliberate and what was not but it didn't matter to her; whether six inches through glass from the bust of Nefertiti or cheek by jowl in a graffiti husk or face to face with all of Georg Baselitz's dogs, she was being remade. All of her courses were in German at a German university, including the sculpture studio and a modernist poetry class supplemented by late-night readings in bars and a drawing class that required alike long afternoons sketching at the Altes Museum and in former bomb shelters. She had worried about sounding stupid in front of the German students but many were much shyer than she was, some also truly brilliant. She enjoyed the ease of their friendship, which shared so few assumptions. She befriended her roommates, also on exchange, from Spain and Croatia and Greece and would go out dancing with them, stopping in bakeries for breakfast before sleeping away a December Sunday's worth of daylight. Then, in the evening, Julienne would go to the studio and work, often the night through. Berlin offered her no shortage of places to be alone, either: sometimes she craved peace and beauty and went to Viktoriapark, high over the city, with a waterfall one could splash in. She secretly thrilled when asked whether she was Dutch or Danish—this meant that she was losing her accent— but moreover she had been given a new brain and body; finally she felt equal with the world.

B ♩

She worked as a temporary paralegal during the week and hostessed in the evening—dabbling in bits of Christmas retail—and was too exhausted to think about anything creative or even to look for stable work. She could hardly read a book on the subway, and whenever Gaspar invited her out to a performance or film or drinks with new composer and musician friends he met in graduate school or simply from having the time to socialize her brain hurt from having to process so much language. When she was without work she found herself no less exhausted, hungry for the next activity that would help to pay their enormous electric bill. That Saturday, with a hundred other people, she would match boxes and boxes of photocopies with their originals in the basement of a law firm to prepare for a deposition in favor of a culpable insurance company. It was possible that they would be asked to stay overnight for twice the pay; the firm would order coffee and cheesecake from Carnegie Deli so that they would stay awake. She decided to spend her lunch break in the park. It was a time of year just dark enough to miss all the daylight. The air was clear and crisp. Two years after graduation, she missed the autumnal rituals of school. Sometimes Julienne liked to pop into the Art Students' League: she felt dumb for thinking so, but it was a beautiful building that

made her feel like she was in France. It seemed to buzz
with all kinds of messy activity, with professionals and
hobbyists and dropouts and dabblers. She went into the
shop. She had forgotten how much she used to enjoy
sensuous materials for their own pleasure but was embarrassed alike to desecrate them in mediocre work and to
leave them untouched, pristine, a waste: airy pigments,
brushes as fine as a deer's eyelashes, mellifluous oils, flu-
vial pens, soft and shimmering pencils. But her favorite
object in the world—a question Gaspar had never asked
of her—was the ordinary kneaded eraser, a glob of rubber
putty to be reshaped again and again; she had even worked
out sculptural compositions on erasers: this had been her
favorite waiting activity at bus stations and doctor's
offices. Julienne bought five of them, in different sizes and
shapes and shades of grayish white. All afternoon, plug-
ging her ears with the same Tokyo String Quartet recording
for the rest of the day because she was not permitted
enough time between legal documents to swap it out, she
imagined spending her time in a different way. She
would wake up early and go to the studio, composing
sculptures of material innovation, imposing scale, and

transformative beauty alongside other artists. She would spend evenings in galleries talking with people who engaged thoughtfully with her and her work. She could go out dancing every weekend because she would not have to work reception at 7 A.M. on Sunday. She would have something to talk about with Gaspar and his friends and colleagues. That night Julienne researched online applications to MFA programs in art: every academic institution in the city seemed to have one. She still had slides from college. Each school asked a hundred dollars for her consideration. Tuition alone would cost thirty thousand dollars a year; she would need to borrow all of it. She would not be able to work full-time; maybe she could model again. Was her German good enough to work as an interpreter? She lightly scratched in these thoughts on a stray page at Gaspar's desk, then kneaded them away.

C ♯

On the subway she sat beside a boy, spiral notebook splayed across his lap, and read from the bold child's handwriting: any time one bounds carbon to a hydroxyl group, alcohol is made. This was also how things worked at Oberschleißheim Bank AG, where Julienne had been working for the previous seven years and one week. Last week the other assistants and receptionists had brought her a small cake, flowers, and a dysfunctional office tchotchke she would need to hide from Jürgen as he would later provide her with another, more expensive dysfunctional office tchotchke probably from silver that she could not hide. Her mother said that Julienne as a third-generation secretary should be so lucky: Julienne's grandmother working at the Anaconda Town Hall in the 1940s could never have dreamed of such a thing. Ought Julienne not to have more respect for feminism; at least it wasn't Secretaries' Day. Her BlackBerry gave a second reminder that there would be demonstrations in Zuccotti Park directly in view of their offices albeit confined directly to the area. Nevertheless, a crowd of observers blocked her usual exit from the subway and she turned around and squiggled vole-like all the way to the J/M/Z platform at Nassau so that by the time she entered the building, a steel SOM box fashioned from Darth Vader's mask, through a utility door left ajar she was already fifteen—and by the time she reached the elevator bank twenty—minutes late. Jürgen was in the back corner. Guten Tag, said Julienne. Jürgen asked, in German, Are you just arriving now? Yes, said Julienne. I'm sorry: I didn't know that the protests would cause such disruption. Jürgen said, You are always fifteen minutes early; thus I asked Bitterfeld Saatzucht to come straight here from the airport. They were at the grains and cereals conference yesterday and have been waiting for nearly one half hour. Julienne apologized again. Jurgen slipped through the elevator crowd without nudging anyone. She was so upset with herself at being late that only when cotton soaked with sweat and melissengeist covered her nose did she understand that she was being asked to take coats.

D ♯

It was far easier to end a sexual dry spell than the crushing eternal nothing her life seemed to have become. The first guy she met was a software engineer from Texas with a beautiful smile who seemed enamored with her but when they went to bed together Julienne thought about anything except for sex, or him: she was out of milk, she had never drawn a swan, she could still make the 6:00 p.m. Iyengar class, maybe she should buy a caulking gun. The bathtub seal was inadequate. She convincingly realized that she had left the stove on, thanked him for a very nice date, and went to Home Depot. The second one was like a golden retriever, which made her feel like she was always being snuck up on. A few weeks later she met Jan, a documentary producer originally from Budapest, with long, bouncy curls and a shy manner. He didn't quite live in New York, he said, but he didn't quite live anywhere. The week before Christmas they saw one another every day. He was observant and polite and sober in the ways that hinted at distant dangerousness. They went out with some friends of his for an impromptu Christmas Eve jazz gig. When they arrived at his home eventually, a large house in Kensington that Jan shared with seven musicians, they tiptoed in, whispering, and laughing like children, peeling off layers of coat and hat and scarf and sweater and sock in the room he rented, which did not have a proper door. The corner was occupied with all sorts of technical equipment, which gave her an uncomfortable flash of familiarity. Involuntary moans fell from her neck and ears and shoulders, like nourishment. Jan took her breast in his mouth and bit the nipple. She made a sound of pain. He pulled at it between his teeth, hard, like a dog grabbing a tea towel in its jaws and snapped it back. She made a screechy sound in the back of her throat. She bit her lip and whimpered. He bit her stomach, her still hollow hip bones, her sex. She began to cry, fully. Jan seemed to interpret this expression as enjoyment. You're not who I want, one side of her brain cried. Mind your own business, Julienne shouted from the other side. I have to do this. Why? Because you have to. This is not for you. It's for me. Look away. Stop, please stop. Shut up! Are you okay? Jan asked. Yes, I'm fine, said Julienne. He seemed so content. The same vertebrae hit the solid plaster again and again. It was the only reminder that she was there.

E ⌐

You were obsessed by *Gulliver's Travels* as a child—and, I guess, *Gargantua and Pantagruel* later on, although you blamed them on Auerbach—but now I know why you were so obsessed by grotesque giants, that they made up so much of your consciousness, had conquered and devoured it over the years of your life. I felt after you broke my nose that you yourself finally felt like a giant: such power! When you died I came to see you face-to-face with the monsters in the snow. What discussions did you have with them before you decided? Did you put up a fight, or did you let go; did you simply surrender? Or—finally having become the giant—did you do it to yourself, feeling so small in that vast boreal forest, deaf to those speaking around you in their secret language, feeling colder than you had ever known, you who loved the warmth of the people in hot places, whom you had lost in the years just before you were lost to the world. You might have done the same thing to me, with less love: all your barbs about my muffled wish to have children, the embedded narcissism and the fulfilment of the female role, that I might have inflated my veins with hormones so that I could birth ten children at once and adopt ten more as a wretched foster mother, and they all would have killed you, an army of Lilliputians, very slowly, at my direction.

I don't know what that joke was about, or why I should so readily have sympathized with your disgust and horror. I had shot back that you seemed to think the fate worse than execution, but it wasn't, and nevertheless what you chose when the monsters finally came for you, the same way they said they would when you were a little boy, when everyone who loved you managed to keep them at bay.

F♮

After the films Julienne couldn't sleep at all: the girls had gone out after the party and came home around four thirty. She made coffee as soon as she saw the sun, up earlier by one hour. She hadn't been to Storm King in years; only once with Leïla—who had hardly permitted her to see anything she wanted to—and although Gaspar had indicated interest several times, he had cracked that he loved nature and that Julienne hated it. She showered and took an entire hour on the subway to reach Port Authority (they were stuck at Clark Street for twenty minutes), then huffed her way onto the bus, where she

dozed against the window till it smacked her head. The
bus let off near the café, from which she purchased an
overpriced ham sandwich and sat with her back to the
South Fields. It was warm out. Julienne noticed that
she was the only person there alone; there was an abundance of babies and small children; she imagined the
logistics of pushing them uphill, on grass, and laughed
aloud about the thought of her mother taking her there
although she had perhaps grown up ninety minutes away
from it, as if she would ever have planned an outing, let
alone one in a vast natural landscape studded with alien
art forms; how dull and stupid Willa would have found the
place, leaving Julienne to climb the forbidden sculptures
so that she could smoke a cigarette or do her nails. This
was a nice place to be a child, she reckoned, despite the
many signs indicating the sculptures weren't to be touched
the directives invoked a dare. It was a place at once pri-
mordial and extraterrestrial, if someone were to film
heaven one might shoot it there: the sculptures—and it
seemed almost crude to call them that—seemed to have
been birthed by the terrain, forming precipices, escarp-
ments, dunes, embankments. She had a soft spot for the

massive, spherical boulders of concrete and fiberglass, burrowed among the trees at the bend in the meadow road, and the massive cliffs' crag, fiberglass and stone, from an artist currently older than time itself, and for the stupefying levity of the suspended steel chunks at a diagonal whose name she could never remember and all the cedar work but her favorite sculptor, her real childhood hero was still Richard Serra, whose contribution sliced the landscape to slowly lay it bare and was everything she understood about vulnerability. Suddenly she remembered a fight they'd had, years earlier, in the moment she noticed that her nose was broken and he had called her baby hungry: it was because he knew that he couldn't stay alive for his own child. Gaspar was gone and could never grow up. It was then that Julienne surrendered to the earth, as if he were in it, and said, over and over again, that she loved him; that she was sorry.

PHOTON SCALE

G

On one hand, she was having a great time. It had been many years since she'd explored a new country; most pieces of public information were in Cantonese and English, but she had never spent time in a city in which she could not make out letters in a sign. She loved archipelagos and most enjoyed the natural beauty available to her; that morning she had taken the tiny, two-hour ferry to Po Toi to bird watch—an activity she had never undertaken, but she purchased some binoculars—and to look at the Bronze Age rock carvings, which reminded her that she was a part of something ancient and intense. That evening she wandered cobbled streets against soft red lights, sampled dishes from egg tart to stinky tofu to morning glory—making notes to seek out these dishes when she returned home—and the next day had been seated for dim sum with a family of seven; when she told them that her father was Chinese, the elderly patriarch read Julienne's nose and ears to dictate that she should marry soon and start a business. She had taken a cable car to Lantau Island to see the giant Buddha statue; taken the rickety wooden tram to the peak; sipped nightcaps in rooftop hotel bars: she had spent hours staring down at the bright, brash city, maybe even the most beautiful she had ever visited, surrounded by hills and volcanoes as if it had bloomed of its own will. She loved the night markets, which had none of the impenetrable sausage fog of food carts in New York. She heard karaoke opera and bought a wind-up cricket for Bob that she thought of keeping for herself. Her heart fluttered and her eyes ahhed. Still, she was resisting it: nothing she saw or did seemed to go beneath the skin; this became evident to her on the way to Guangzhou during which she was seated opposite the direction of the train: the smog after Shen-zhen station cosseted the train so that she might have been in a rain cloud—factories everywhere! She had never seen such crowded buildings; laundry draped the balconies of tower blocks, dried and dirtied by the force of the train. Around Dongguan she saw rivers of cans, then rivers of plastic bottles, then rivers of paper; work-ers stood barefoot in the calf-deep water, raking them apart, separating detritus under the thick sky. When tears sprang at her eyes she wanted to slap her own wrist: had this been a mistake or a vacation; was her father from here or perhaps his parents—were they the sort to till the cans or just the sort to make demands? (This rhymed.)

A ♩

Gaspar kept a black Post-it note on his high school year-book that read GASPAR'S LABORATORY in metallic ink and was spattered in shiny, hand-drawn bombs. He chuckled and said: My parents were working outside the States for much of the early nineties and I didn't care for my school in Connecticut so decided to go to boarding school. To me it looked like summer camp, all year long, but bigger, anyway, than the college my mom teaches at, probably as many students; there were two museums on campus, a good music program, and required sports that I found vaguely exotic. Everyone was nicer than I expected, not that there weren't hazing incidents, but I guess I escaped the asshole dorms. Anyway, my room was obviously super messy—as you know, sorry; I like to think it was worse then—wires everywhere from music, or physics class, or to dig out the innards of my computer when it didn't work so my friend in the room next door was always heckling me about it and made this sticker which he put on my door. I thought it was funny and never took it down. Anyway, there was a class on *Paradise Lost* normally taught by a great teacher who went on sabbatical in Rome so we got this jerk from the development office who had done his college thesis on Milton. He was really lame: once as a special event he forced us all to go to his house in a van so that we could eat sandwiches from the cafeteria in his living room, which was literally all beige and free of décor except for some children's crayon scribbles Scotch-taped to the wall and three living room sofas literally filled with Popples—do you remember them? They were like pink monkeys that you could tuck into themselves so that they could become marsupials. Maybe it was a *Gremlins* riff. But we all had to sit on the floor because everything was covered in Popples. It just occurred to me that he might not have had a kid at all. Anyway, I'm not totally sure what I did to anger him, so I stopped talking during class hoping it would chill him out, but that made him even more irritated. So he starts going around to my advisor, other teachers, other people in music or my dorm or lacrosse, trying to find out my deal, I guess. Also I was trying to grow a beard for fun because the novelty of shaving had worn off. It was enough of a terrorist vibe, I thought at first, for him to report me to the administration, but my grades were fine except for the ones he gave me, and most anecdotal evidence revealed me to be a stand-up young man, just gawky and nervous, you know? But then there was an investigation, one I wasn't allowed to know about until the fucking FBI showed up. So there must have been something, I guess, that no one was willing to tell me about, but of enough severity that they didn't just tell the guy to fuck off. Like I'm probably not the only sixteen-year-old ever to be questioned by the FBI but it was rare enough to be super awkward at best. My parents were furious and told me to withdraw but I thought that would confirm their suspicions and everyone else including the head of school who didn't even know me was like, Gaspar is not a terrorist, dude. Also, I liked my life there—couldn't he leave instead if he was so afraid that I'd blow up his Popples? Anyway, we all became American citizens that summer without raising any flags, which should tell you everything you need to know about regular application of policy but I'm sure they're still watching everything we do. Anyway, the teacher wouldn't apologize and I refused to attend his class so it was negotiated that I could stop going and submit my work in his mailbox—he gave me the equivalent of, like, a D—and after that I only saw him once, when I was carrying a huge box of test tubes from my advisor's apartment to the science building. I said hi, but he just stared at me till I waggled my eyebrows and heard him gasp audibly.

B

Eventually Julienne's use of composite plastic fiberglass-reinforced polyesters became a running gag: it was strange that she rejected more workable materials despite her lack of skill, critics often remarked, but by the time she finished her degree Julienne had at least acquired a technical mastery of the material; many suggested that the works resembled the gardening sculptures of different unfashionable relatives, which might have been leveraged creatively for comment; the real issue, however, was an inherent lack of conceptual intelligence, her professor said at the final thesis show, any sense of scale or proportion, intent. Talent, obviously, he summarized to the visiting critics and the sixty or so students present. She has no fucking talent. What can you do? At home—having nothing to celebrate at the reception after the review—she told Gaspar about the incident; he said that the professor was obviously a dick and a horrible teacher. Gaspar always knew the right thing to say; he had been dedicated, as a young musician, and had been shouted away from auditions in primary school. It's only them, he explained, managing to blot her tears without poking her eyes. They worry about their own failures and the things they like or don't like as verdicts upon their own lives. What should I do? she asked. Go to the studio, he said, and start again. Three years later, during which Julienne hadn't made a thing, she had been given the afternoon off after accompanying Jürgen to a client meeting and went into some of the gallery buildings on Fifty-Seventh Street. She discovered, to her chagrin, that her thesis professor's gallery was showing his latest works (she no longer kept up with such happenings), and in the back was a massive cobweb of glistening fiberglass. She gasped: caught within it was a mass of student work, bits of study model, but also remnants from several of Julienne's final pieces from the show, which she had put into the trash. The catalog text read: the utterly miraculous *Cat's Cradle* catches within its mesh large chunks of debris and works of forsaken outsider art, a meditation on power, inequality, the nature of borders, and revolution.

C

Julienne's nose was still swollen from the lightbulb incident—there seemed to be a rumor at work that she had a rhinoplasty; her German was very good but still not enough to understand the nuances of murmured slang from newly expatriated youths; nevertheless, eine Nase war eine Nase: she prayed that it would heal normally. To smooth things over, she asked some of the girls—and they were always girls, no matter their ages—to go for drinks after work. They chose a cocktail bar in the East Village with the word experimental in its name but Julienne sampled the girls' drinks and they all tasted of strawberry chewing gum. She chose something with Lillet Blanc and lemongrass and decided to limit herself to blended scotches should there be a second round. Outside of work she spoke English with her colleagues: the conversations were very different from the ones she might have with Jennifer, Leïla, or Maggie; some of the younger ones had come to America to travel and spoke about weekends in Charleston, a place they found charming but scary, or weeks of their generous vacation time spent in Banff or Tulum, but mostly these girls only talked about their husbands—none of them had children. Julienne wondered whether they had formed the habit at work: their bankers were work husbands and their husbands were just husbands and there was just no time for anything else. In a way she understood—having lived with Gaspar longer than any of them had been married—but she did not want to talk about him with anyone except for him. Did that make sense? she asked them. They stared at her for a second and began talking about a trip to Charleston with their husbands. Julienne texted Gaspar to ask where he was. He was talking to a fellow musician at a bar named for the proletariat in Cooper Square. His work was so different from hers. She told him to come by. When he arrived he squeezed into the booth next to Julienne and introduced himself to the girls. From then on their attention was rapt. Everything that Gaspar did was fascinating; perhaps Julienne was simply jaded: he was attractive, charming, interested in others, a successful artist, well-mannered. No, she thought. These were simply people that he didn't know, unspoiled by his acquaintance. Afterward, waiting for the subway,

Gaspar remarked, all of your friends talk very fast. Julienne said, They're German: so many ideas to express concisely. No, Gaspar said, your American friends do the same thing. Leïla doesn't, said Julienne. Well, that doesn't count, he said. Because you want to be her husband. Let's never drink again, said Julienne. She went into a separate car when the train arrived.

D

How had Julienne come to clean offices, and then homes? After the firing she began temp work and to apply for other executive assistant jobs in finance but the thought of being shackled to another MD—to be work wife to yet another married middle-aged man with children—without even being able to keep up her German made her feel ill. She preferred no longer to sit at a desk. When she went to interview with the cleaning agencies she felt badly: it was one of the few jobs non-English speakers could take with a reasonable wage. Still, the work suited her: she was naturally fastidious, loathed dirt—untended houseplants made her cringe—and it was an honest day's labor. She had already temped in most of the midtown office buildings she was contracted to clean and was amused to see what had changed, as well as the nuances of what she was expected to manage, being delicate around soundproofed walls and the ubiquitous Eames bucket chair. When she tidied private offices and removed trash from cubicle wastebaskets the details amused her, children's drawings but also furious scratches on documents. Cleaning the bathrooms on the first few days brought up such fury and degradation—was this her station, to clean the literal excrement of the bourgeoisie, as she had often felt in the weeks following Gaspar's departure—but then she began to find the work almost therapeutic; she imagined that she was washing and scrubbing away all that she found vulgar about this world. She had to sign a waiver concerning all the chemical exposure but truthfully she found synthetics bracing and strong. Her young housemates liked to use fragrant, insipid, organic products in the kitchen and bathroom and sometimes, before cooking or showering, Julienne would spray down everything with bleach and start again. If she cleaned houses during the day and offices in the evening, with the occasional weekend of temp work, Julienne estimated that she would be able to replace her previous salary (although, of course, without insurance or retirement benefits and having to pay self-employment tax). She placed an ad on Craigslist—no one would check references if she priced her labor lowly enough—she had enough gigs on the Upper East Side to fill a Tuesday. The list of tasks left to cleaners was astonishing and better suited to those with construction or landscape training: one person asked her to ensure that the asphalt on the roof deck was curing properly; if not, could she please mix a bit of lime into the mixture in the plastic barrel and pour it in very thin layers? As well, lime was good for plant soil; could she please dust it with the stuff to scatter away insects. Julienne considered the logic, drying out the insects, drying out the soil. There was a drought already: who would want such a thing? Some of the apartments were massive, three or four floors sectioned into a tower; sometimes the entire floorplate of an historic coop: rich people were so cheap, she thought, having posted the lowest wage she saw online. Still, she was meticulous in her work and in thrall to the sensuous materials, however clichéd, like French oak in a herringbone pattern: someone had chosen to chop down oak trees in France, dry the wood, treat the wood, prepare the wood into refined plank shapes, finish the wood, send the wood to the US, hope that someone would know how to install the wood correctly, thousands of times. When asked to hand polish the floors she was at first secretly annoyed but in due course this became her favored task, washing them gently with soap, drying them with clean cloths, buffing them lightly, sealing them with wax. Julienne thought that the floors' owners might become friends of hers (some may even have gone to college with her, she reckoned), were something unfortunate to happen in their lives.

E ⌐

I have something embarrassing to tell you, which is that at the start of graduate school, when I had the idea that I should be exorcising my demons in every throwaway exercise, I would find different ways to channel you into being, not your essence, but very literally your form and textures, as if I would forget to find you in a crowd. The more I learned about you, the less of an idea I had of who you were, but that does not compare to what I feel now. It was deranged behavior, in hindsight: I would begin to carve your hands and wind up with an anemone; your nose would end in the tetrahedron I had started with for simple reasons—I had the capacity to make and to destroy you and you had the very same powers over me. You were tall and skinny back then, like glass. You preferred to buy milk in glass bottles; your mother is a mathematician, not the sort to worry about such things, but she fed you well and would never bore you with those matters. Your father was a person of great care; I knew not to take it personally when he was kind to me. Every time we visited your house, I marveled at all the glass-work, the old panes he had set into your new home, like harvested organs, the patterns he designed for the addition, and the studio out back, after Persian geometries studied at his grandparents' knees. You are becoming translucent to me: I might still grow old, but you certainly will not, and maybe someday I will know what your son looks like when he's your age. In the photographs I have left from your life, only your face seems to dissolve with time, the imprint that is yours alone.

F

In the months that followed Gaspar's passing—ruled a suicide, to the public—Julienne had come to reside in the space of the undead. She made sure to smile brightly for her roommates, who still gathered with college friends for cooking competitions, charades, charity races, and so on. She was especially diligent in cleaning. Her bedroom locked with a key and she would lie there, not sleeping, all night, until it was time to bathe and to go to work. She was doing maternity coverage in a boutique investment bank and performed fifteen minutes of labor each day. She did not sleep or eat anything for one full week after receiving the news and often drank herbal tea to suppress the rare twinge of appetite; all food seemed to glow with poison. Her constitution was like the innards of a plane crash, gasoline-plump veins wound round a fiery skeleton of crushed glass; to face the world she locked and loaded herself in a diving bell, having become the picture of stony stillness; when a man tried to knock her out of his way it was he who fell to the subway platform, clutching his elbow in pain. At work she had nothing to pay attention to and nothing could take her attention: during her lunch breaks she went to the privately owned public atrium and stared at things: empty fountains, the vastness of the bracketed ceiling above, the continuous flat black granite that had rendered the building a mausoleum. She did not want to bury him here; she wished herself into the stone instead.

G

Her last stop in mainland China before flying home from Hong Kong was in Guangxi Province. She had landed in Guilin in the early morning and stayed in an austere, very clean room booked through a government-sponsored agency in Guangzhou. Only a Chinese-language tour was available but she was told that it wouldn't matter; one could never hear the guides anyway. She started studying the characters and names of cities: Guang meant expanse.

After checking in, she would travel to the rice terraces in Longsheng; springtime was the perfect season to visit, she was assured. Then she would follow the Li River, famous for its massive slabs of karst, visible on the twenty yuan note, said the travel agent. The bus ride took them up slowly, over a steep spiral till she could see the finely curved terraces, sliced into the landscape seven hundred years earlier, still in use; water fell from the top of the hill down a stepped system of walled-in basins. The walk as well was very steep and narrow; she stopped to let dogs pass and sometimes felt she might fall. For lunch she had a large plate of pea shoots and straw mushrooms, grown on the hill. She watched a woman, hunched over, wearing red lipstick, and felt that she was seeing something of her own future. The boat trip from Guilin to Yangshuo was in the afternoon. She couldn't, of course, understand the guide. Some people asked her to pose with them in a photograph, which made her feel sad. When they could go to the top deck she did. She admired the texture of the rock, eroded through time, and the blankness of the limestone faces, nevertheless able to support massive trees.

Julienne became distracted by a dragonfly on a woman's shoulder. Their tourist boat was the loudest thing around. Rowers stood on bamboo rafts that sailed beside them and cormorants soared above their heads. In shadow they seemed translucent.

NOTES

The musical scales that structure each chapter are based loosely on the Arabic melodic structure known as the maqam and here used to indicate time: events in A take place between 1979 and 2000; B between 2000 and 2010; C between 2010 and 2011; D between 2012 and 2015; E direct address; F between 2015 and 2016; G in 2016.

Page 1: Guillaume Apollinaire, "Zone" (1913) in *Alcools*, (Gallimard 1950).

Page 6: Freeman Dyson, "Birds and Frogs" (2010) In *The Best Writing on Mathematics 2010* edited by Mircea Pitici, 57–78. Princeton: Princeton University Press, 2011.

Page 17: Eija-Liisa Ahtila, "Consolation Service" (2000), in *Video via Venice: Highlights from the Biennale*, Institute of Contemporary Arts, Boston, April 26–July 2, 2000.

Page 20: Sibylle Berg, *Das Unerfreuliche zuerst: Herrengeschichten*, (KiWi-Taschenbuch, 2001).

NOTES

Page 26: Maurice Ravel, *Gaspard de la Nuit: Trois poèmes pour piano d'après Aloysius Bertrand* (Durand, 2007, originally published 1909).

Page 50: "Episode 1.7; Hotel La Rut 1–3," (1989), *The Kids in the Hall*, created by Dave Foley, Bruce McCulloch, Kevin McDonald, Mark McKinney, and Scott Thompson.

Page 73: *Farewell, My Concubine*, directed by Kaige Chen, with performances by Leslie Cheung, Fengyi Zhang, Gong Li (Miramax, 1993).

Page 98: Elizabeth Alexander, *The Light of the World* (Grand Central Publishing, 2016).

Page 99: "Syrian Refugees in Turkey Remain Defiant," *Al Jazeera*, November 26, 2011.

Page 110: Alvin Lucier, *Music 109* (Wesleyan University Press, 2012).

Page 123: *The Deep Blue Sea*, directed by Terence Davies, with performances by Rachel Weisz, Tom Hiddleston, Simon Russell Beale (Paramount, 2012).

Page 131: Sigmund Freud, *On the History of the Psycho-Analytic Movement* (W. W. Norton, 1990).

NOTES

Page 142: *Hiroshima Mon Amour*, directed by Alain Resnais, with performances by Emmanuelle Riva, Eiji Okada (Cocinor, 1959).

Page 157: Richard Serra. *Verb List*. 1967. The Museum of Modern Art, New York.

Page 163. *The Disappearance of Eleanor Rigby*, directed by Ned Benson, with performances by Jessica Chastain, James McAvoy, Viola Davis. (The Weinstein Company, 2014).

Page 165. Tim Fetherston, "Forced solar gazing-a common technique of torture?," *Eye (London, England)* vol. 34, 10 (2020): 1820–1824.

Page 170. Jacques Roubaud, *The Great Fire of London: A Story with Interpolations and Bifurcations*, translated by Dominic Di Bernardi (Dalkey Archive Press, 2005).

ACKNOWLEDGMENTS

I am profoundly grateful to my agent, Akin Akinwumi, and to my editors, Ben Schrank and Signe Swanson, who saw that this work merited its own covers and helped me to cut up and reassemble it again and again into a real book. Their patience, intelligence, and creativity are jewels in this world.

Exuberant thanks to the readers who provided this work with brilliant and kindhearted attention: Madeleine Moss, Stephanie Davy, Hannah Flood, and Angela Cartier, and to Penn Whaling for her advice in publishing.

Sincere appreciation to the MFA Program at Washington University in St. Louis, without whose largesse this work would not have been written, especially to Marshall Klimasewiski, in whose course this work was drafted, and to Mary Jo Bang and Carl Phillips, in whose courses respectively the sections and structure of the book were developed, as well as to Micheline Aharonian Marcom, who offered thoughtful feedback on the piece.

ABOUT THE AUTHOR

Monica Datta received degrees in architecture and urban design from the City University of New York, the London School of Economics, and the Bartlett School of Architecture (UCL), as well as an MFA in creative writing from Washington University in St. Louis. Her writing has appeared in *Conjunctions, The Rupture/The Collagist, Blackbird, The New Inquiry,* and other journals. She teaches at Pratt Institute.

Astra House and the author would like to credit those who worked on the publication of this book. The team at Astra House would like to thank everyone who helped to publish *Thieving Sun*.

PUBLISHER
Ben Schrank

EDITORIAL
Signe Swanson

PUBLICITY
Rachael Small
Alexis Nowicki

MARKETING
Tiffany Gonzalez
Sarah Christensen Fu

SALES
Jack W. Perry

DESIGN
Jacket: Rodrigo Corral Studio
Interior: Alissa Theodor
Frances DiGiovanni

PRODUCTION
Lisa Taylor
Elizabeth Koehler

MANAGING EDITORIAL
Alisa Trager
Olivia Dontsov

COPYEDITING & PROOFREADING
Janine Barlow
John Vasile

COMPOSITION
Westchester Publishing Services